"I'm with you till the end, Adriana. However long it takes until we catch him."

But there could be another end to this story—she knew that better than anyone.

"I'll keep you safe. I swear."

"What about the ... he the last time?"

His mouth quirk ... lf smile she was st ... 's going to make m...

Oh, my.

"Okay." She barely realized she'd agreed to his protection until the word shot out of her mouth, against her better judgment. He didn't deserve to be involved in this. He didn't deserve to die because of her.

As if he could read her thoughts, something softened in his deep hazel eyes. He reached up to trace her jawline with his hand, making the barest contact with her skin. It stole her breath all the same....

TRACY MONTOYA

I'LL BE WATCHING YOU

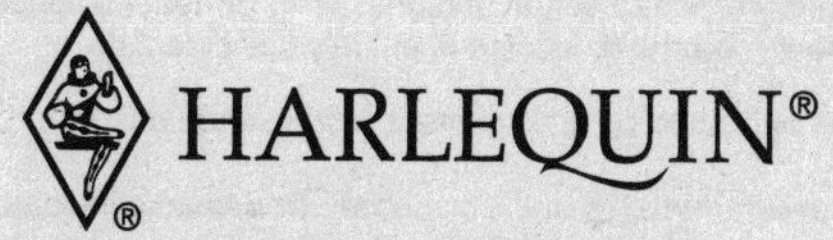

TORONTO • NEW YORK • LONDON
AMSTERDAM • PARIS • SYDNEY • HAMBURG
STOCKHOLM • ATHENS • TOKYO • MILAN • MADRID
PRAGUE • WARSAW • BUDAPEST • AUCKLAND

To Kim Fisk. You earned this one with all of those blitz critiques I made you do! I'm blessed to have you for a friend.

ISBN-13: 978-0-373-88831-3
ISBN-10: 0-373-88831-7

I'LL BE WATCHING YOU

This edition published by arrangement with Harlequin Books S.A.

www.eHarlequin.com

Printed in U.S.A.

ABOUT THE AUTHOR

Tracy Montoya is a magazine editor for a crunchy nonprofit in Washington, D.C., though at present she's telecommuting from her house in Seoul, Korea. She lives with a psychotic cat, a lovable yet daft lhasa apso and a husband who's turned their home into the Island of Lost/Broken/Strange-Looking Antiques. A member of the National Association of Hispanic Journalists and the Society of Environmental Journalists, Tracy has written about everything from Booker Prize–winning poet Martín Espada to socially responsible mutual funds to soap opera summits. Her articles have appeared in a variety of publications, such as *Hope, Utne Reader, Satya, YES!, Natural Home* and *New York Naturally.* Prior to launching her journalism career, she taught in an under-resourced school in Louisiana through the AmeriCorps Teach for America program.

Tracy holds a master's degree in English literature from Boston College and a BA in the same from St. Mary's University. When she's not writing, she likes to scuba dive, forget to go to kickboxing class, wallow in bed with a good book, or get out her guitar with a group of friends and pretend she's Suzanne Vega.

She loves to hear from readers—e-mail TracyMontoya@aol.com or visit www.tracymontoya.com.

Books by Tracy Montoya

HARLEQUIN INTRIGUE

750—MAXIMUM SECURITY
877—HOUSE OF SECRETS*
883—NEXT OF KIN*
889—SHADOW GUARDIAN*
986—FINDING HIS CHILD
1032—TELLING SECRETS
1057—I'LL BE WATCHING YOU

*MISSION: FAMILY

CAST OF CHARACTERS

Adriana Torres—Four years ago, Adriana's fiancé was killed in the line of duty while hunting serial killer Elijah Carter. Now someone is leaving her mysterious threats, and dredging up all of her long-buried painful memories.

Daniel Cardenas—The Monterey police detective is determined to keep Adriana safe from the stalker whose threats seem to be escalating—even while she's determined to shut him out.

Elijah Carter—A vicious serial killer whose struggle with police and FBI resulted in his falling into the dangerous waters lining Monterey Bay. His body was never found.

Stan Peterson—Adriana's yoga student seems to have an unhealthy interest in his teacher.

James Brentwood—The Monterey police detective—and Adriana's fiancé—was shot and killed by Elijah Carter.

Liz Borkowski—Daniel's no-nonsense partner and Adriana's friend, Detective Borkowski well remembers Elijah Carter, because she almost died under his knife.

A.J. Lockwood—The veteran detective knows Elijah Carter's killing methods well—and he's convinced Carter survived and is back to kill again.

Sean Cantrell—Could Adriana's teenage neighbor be behind the threats left at her door?

Prologue

Stifling a yawn with his fist, Detective Daniel Cardenas wondered not for the first time what the hell he was doing up at oh-dark-hundred in the morning, several hours before his shift was supposed to start. His dashboard clock read 3:07 a.m. as he maneuvered his unmarked Crown Victoria slowly through the gauntlet of blue-and-whites lining East Alvarado Street, their flashing lights creating an eerie, pulsing red halo around the small neighborhood. It was normally considered one of Monterey, California's, "safer" areas.

Not tonight, obviously.

When his partner had called him down here, she hadn't bothered to give him any details. But something in her normally no-nonsense voice had sent his cop sense into overdrive, and he knew it was shut-up-and-go time. So he shut up, hung up and went. All without his usual morning jolt of caffeine.

God, he would have sawed off his right arm for some coffee.

Pulling his car alongside the curb, about a block away from the small shotgun-style bungalow at the center of all the activity, Daniel got out and made his way back toward 447 East Alvarado. Radio chatter had indicated a homicide had taken place, and from the fact that every cop in the metro area and then some seemed to be parked on this one street, it wasn't going to be a pretty one.

He walked under a streetlight, and the sudden brightness of its tungsten lamp shining down upon him made his head throb. Ahead, some neighborhood residents huddled together in a tight, worried-looking group, occasionally craning their necks or shuffling from side to side to see what was going on. Unfortunately for them, an ambulance with two very jittery-looking EMTs leaning against it blocked their view. As if sensing his approach, one of the women onlookers turned around and broke away from the group when she saw him.

"Excuse me," the woman said, tightly clutching the lapels of her ratty red bathrobe together with one hand. "Are you with the police? Because I didn't know the girls who lived there well, but..."

"Ma'am, at this point, I don't know any more than you do," he said politely. "But—"

"It's our right to know," she said, falling into step beside him. "Our taxes pay your salary, young man. I won't—"

Without breaking his stride, Daniel slanted a cool look at her.

"Oh, well, I—" Patting her hair, she scurried back among her friends, the rest of her statement hanging unfinished in the air. He wasn't allowed to dole out any information to people who weren't next of kin this early in the game. And he definitely wasn't spilling his guts to the neighborhood gossip at any point. They were pretty much the only ones who tried to play the we-pay-your-taxes card.

Then again, if she'd come at him with a double-shot espresso, he might have been persuaded to make something up on the spot.

As he approached the yellow tape that cordoned off the scene, a street cop strode across the front yard to meet him, backlit by one of the homicide squad's portable spotlights. Daniel flashed his badge, then ducked under the tape without waiting for the guy's blessing. As expected, the uniform gave him a curt nod and backed off.

"Cardenas!"

A. J. Lockwood, a seasoned detective who'd been with the MPD since the beginning of time, bounded down the home's front steps and crossed the yard to Daniel. Judging from his expression, whatever was inside was going to be bad. Generally, the grislier the scene, the blacker Lockwood's dark sense of humor became. But tonight the man's ever-present sardonic grin was nowhere in sight.

Not a kid. Please don't let it have been a kid.

"Janie Sanchez, graduate student at the Language Institute," Lockwood said in greeting, not even bothering with normal pleasantries like "hello" or "you look like hell."

"She's our homicide?" Daniel asked.

"Oh, yeah." Lockwood's square jaw clenched and worked, but instead of launching into a description of the scene, he merely narrowed his flinty gaze at Daniel. "So what do you look so chipper for? I've been up for an hour now, and I still feel like hell. Borkowski says she got ahold of you, like, two minutes ago, and you look as if you were lying in bed in that suit, waiting for someone to call."

Truth was he felt about as chipper as a pile of roadkill. An uncaffeinated pile of roadkill.

Then again, he'd long ago realized that what was going on inside his head didn't often show up on his face, whether he realized it or not.

"Who's that over there in the bushes?" Daniel asked, jerking his head toward the cop bent over the shrubbery a few feet away, making the most god-awful noises.

"Rookie. He's been yakking all over the place since he got here."

Great, one of *those* cases. "That bad?"

Lockwood gave a small grunt that would have been a short laugh under normal circumstances. "Worse. *I* felt like yakking. Don't tell anyone." He glanced back at the house's open doorway, which was blocked by a short, stocky uniform who looked like a human fireplug, standing guard. Someone had drawn the curtains inside.

"It's..." Lockwood blew out a long, slow puff of air. "Damn, Cardenas, I think he's back."

With that one sentence, the fatigue Daniel felt abruptly vanished. There was only one "he" in their shared history on the force—maybe even in the history of the entire city—that could make a rookie lose his breakfast and put the fear of God into a veteran like Lockwood.

Impossible.

Pushing past Lockwood without so much as a goodbye, he propelled himself through the small mass of his colleagues milling around outside, past the cluster of EMTs standing around with nothing to do. Taking the three front steps in two strides, he entered the house, all but ignoring the crime-scene techs taking flash photographs in the front sitting room as he followed the noise to the living room in the middle.

The few detectives in the room parted like the Red Sea when he entered, revealing his grim-faced partner standing over a body. Detective Liz Borkowski looked up as he approached, her normally pale, Irish-and-Polish complexion gone as white as bone.

"Five-point ligature marks on the ankles, wrists and neck," one of the crime-scene techs murmured from a few feet away, obligingly describing the horror in the room to another tech who held a video camera.

Janie Sanchez's body lay sprawled out on a blood-soaked rug in front of the living room's brick fireplace. She'd been deliberately posed in a demeaning, spread-eagle fashion, her head tilted to the side, giving her the look of a broken marionette. Her glassy, unseeing eyes stared at something beyond the ceiling.

He'd seen this all before. He could have described the scene to the crime lab's video camera with his eyes closed.

Because he still dreamed about the others. They all did.

"...fishing line still wrapped around the victim's ankles and wrists..." The tech's monotone was the only sound in the room besides everyone else's breathing. "...defensive wounds on her hands..."

The vulnerable, taut skin on Janie's bare stomach had been carved through repeatedly with a knife that had left her abdomen raw and mutilated.

Somebody's sister. Somebody's daughter.

"...multiple lacerations on her body, concentrated mostly on her abdominal area, where they appear to be in a gridlike pattern..."

Detach. He had to forget about who she'd been, and focus on who had killed her.

But how did you tell someone their daughter, their sister, their friend and neighbor had been killed by a ghost?

A ghost that hadn't walked for four years.

Where've you been, Elijah Carter?

The newspapers had come up with a more colorful name for the man who'd stalked and killed eleven women, who'd crossed the country from Louisiana and California, escalating until the last few had died not mercifully or quickly, but a long, slow, torturous death he wouldn't have wished on the worst of criminals. They called him The Surgeon. Because he liked to carve up women in his special, singular, painstaking way.

Daniel refused to call him that. Whatever he was, he was still just a man.

A man who'd apparently risen from the dead.

He crouched down beside Janie and found himself staring at one of her hands. Her slim fingers curled slightly upward, tipped with bubblegum-pink, carefully tended nails that were now caked with blood. Her wrists were red and swollen from where he'd tied them.

He looked at her face. She'd been a pretty girl.

Somebody's sister. Somebody's daughter.

"Who found the body?" he asked Liz, as she knelt down beside him.

"Roommate," she said, her voice slightly hoarse. "She's outside."

"…multiple lacerations to the abdomen, cuts most likely made with a serrated-edge blade," the tech droned on.

Serrated edge. Because Elijah Carter liked to rip, not slice.

"What do you think, Liz?" he asked quietly, and every person in the room strained to hear his partner's answer. Along with Lockwood, the two of them had been on the special FBI-Monterey PD task force four years ago that had cornered Elijah Carter on the rock-strewn shores of the Pacific Ocean. They'd been down this damn road before.

Something small and vulnerable flickered across his partner's face. She was probably thinking of her own daughters, one just a couple of years younger than Janie Sanchez.

"Copycat." She lifted her head to look him square in the eye. "Unofficially speaking." She pointed with a latex-gloved hand to the victim's torn-up stomach. "Carter used to carve a very precise grid into his victims. Three lines down, four across."

She would know.

"This victim has four lines down, four across. And that's not the only thing that's off." Borkowski bent down to trace a finger gently along the vicious bruising across the young woman's neck.

"That looks as if someone strangled her with a strap of some sort," Daniel said, crouching down on the other side of the body. "Carter liked to use his hands."

"Exactly."

"Signatures can change over time, Borkowski. Sure we have some variation, but the overall theme is still there."

Signatures were behaviors that went beyond what was necessary to commit a crime, and fulfilled a killer's twisted psychological needs. Repeatedly strangling his victims and reviving them was one of Carter's signature behaviors. Cutting that grid into her abdomen was a signature behavior. He'd changed things up a bit, but it still might be Elijah Carter. Or, as Borkowski obviously hoped, it might not.

"The M.E. will have to tell us for sure, but I think she may have been sexually assaulted, too," Liz said. "Carter never did that. That would change his MO. Which just doesn't happen."

Daniel made a point to keep his focus steady on the contusions on Janie Sanchez's neck. It seemed like another violation to look at the rest of her body while having this discussion.

"Dammit, Cardenas, it *has* to be a copycat."

He jerked his head up in surprise—his tough-as-nails partner never let her emotions show. Not like that—imposing her own interpretation on a crime scene because she couldn't bear to think of the alternative.

She didn't meet his eye, instead rising from the ground. Squaring her shoulders, she came back to herself and started barking orders. She swept from the room, and everyone else hustled to comply with her commands, obviously relieved to have something to occupy their too-busy minds.

As Daniel rose, Lockwood approached him.

"Up until 1905, it was legal in China to execute someone for a capital offense by *lingchi*, or the 'death of a thousand cuts,'" Lockwood murmured as he, too, stared down at the body.

Daniel knew what he was talking about. The ancient form of capital punishment was reportedly as gruesome as the name suggested, with the executioner inflicting multiple nonlethal cuts all over the victim's body, prolonging death until said victim finally expired from his cumulative wounds.

"Janie Sanchez died of a thousand cuts," Lockwood continued. "Borkowski might want to insist it's a copycat, but I don't know…I've never seen another man who did *that* to his victims."

Chapter One

Hustling out the door on her way to work, Adriana Torres caught a glimpse of something out of the corner of her eye that stopped her in her tracks. Her keys fell out of her suddenly slack grip, jangling loudly as they hit the ground.

A nasty-looking hunting knife protruded from her home's siding. Pinned to the wood by the sharply gleaming steel was a folded slip of paper. She didn't need to read its contents to know that the message would be very concise and very disturbing.

"Nice."

Some people's neighbors said good morning to each other as they started their day. Hers jabbed knives into her house. And *por el amor de Dios,* what had her house ever done to them?

Rolling her eyes heavenward and muttering a brief prayer for patience in Spanish, Addy grabbed hold of the handle, giving it a good tug. When it didn't come out on the first try, she dropped her tote back on her front stoop with a thud and tried again with both hands until the knife chunked free.

She didn't bother to glance around her quiet street, figuring it was hardly worth it to muster up the energy to be annoyed anymore. As one of the neighborhood dogs started up a faraway, staccato bark, she examined the latest addition to her growing collection of cutlery. It felt heavier and looked a little more expensive than usual.

Whatever. Maybe the idiot who'd put it there thought that spending more money would be scarier. As if.

Purposefully adopting a bored expression, just in case the nasty little twerp was watching, she picked up her keys and dropped them back into her purse. She'd always hated the thought of living in a wealthy gated community, but at times like this the idea had its attractions.

Pushing the door back open with one hip, she kicked at the slip of paper that had fallen to the ground after she'd freed the knife holding it. It fluttered inside the house, and she picked up her tote and followed suit. Without bothering to pick the paper up, she headed for the phone in her kitchen. She dialed the familiar number without glancing at the list of her favorite contacts stuck to the fridge.

"Borkowski," came a woman's curt response.

"Hey, Liz, it's me." Addy leaned against the counter, a frisson of annoyance tracking up her spine as she contemplated being late to work because of a stupid prank…again. But while she and Liz both knew that none of the teenage troublemakers who lived on her block was going to slink forward and confess, she'd promised her friend she would call each and every time someone stabbed her house. "Got another note."

"Same deal as last time?"

Addy tossed the knife on the counter. "If by that you mean, one large, ugly knife that left yet another large, ugly hole in my siding, yes. Every time Halloween comes around, it's the prank du jour."

Liz swore softly—which was very uncharacteristic of her—and for the first time, Addy realized that the usual sounds she heard in the background when she called Liz at the station—papers shuffling, phones ringing—

weren't present. Instead, it sounded like Liz was outside.

"Is this a bad time?" Addy asked. "You out and about doing your cop thing?"

"No, no," said Liz, sounding somewhat preoccupied despite her denial. "I'm at a scene, but this is important."

"After seven of these notes since…" She let her voice trail off, not wanting to think about the event that had divided her life into *before* and *since.* "I don't think it's all that important, Liz. The sky hasn't fallen yet."

The first threat had also come in October, exactly a year after the love of Addy's life, Monterey Police Detective James Brentwood, had been killed in the line of duty while hunting a prolific serial killer—a serial killer who was now dead, thank you very much. But a bestselling book about the case had made her little corner of the city rather notorious, since the killer known as The Surgeon had drowned just a few yards away from Addy's home in an FBI-Monterey PD undercover operation.

And suddenly the kids in her neighborhood had found it amusing to leave notes on her door, pretending to be the resurrected killer of her beloved fiancé by mimicking his favorite way of terrorizing his intended victims.

Sometimes you just had to wonder what was wrong with people.

The first time, the message had terrified her beyond belief, coming on the grim anniversary as it had. Then, more notes came, and they were always the same—someone would leave a cheap knife embedded in her wooden door, along with a childishly scrawled note saying he was "coming for" her.

So she'd bought a security system and a steel front door, and the notes kept coming, until there had been so many, all they sparked in her was contempt. If someone was really out to get her, she figured they'd have done something by now, rather than simply continuing to write about it. And on one occasion, she'd seen a suspiciously gangly, teenager-looking shadow lurking about her front door when another note had appeared, which had led her and the police to believe that she was merely the target of a few young pranksters in the area with tragically inept parents.

"I'm sorry, Addy," Liz said, breaking a silence that had stretched out for too long. It seemed as if all of her conversations did that, in the four years since James had died. "This has to be so hard on you, especially now."

Especially now. October again. The month when she'd lost James.

Addy picked at a hangnail as she watched the cold waves of the Pacific Ocean crash spectacularly against the jagged black rocks that lined the shore outside her window. Four years. She'd gotten to the point where she could handle being left behind most days, where the intense, indescribable grief she'd felt at losing him was just a dull memory, hanging in the background of her everyday activities—always there, but something she could live with. Like Liz lived with it, although she and James had just been work partners and friends.

And then sometimes, out of the blue, it sucker-punched Addy in the stomach, leaving her gasping for air and wondering whether she'd even be able to function into the next hour, much less the next decade. And all the ones that would come after.

Too long. Too long to be without him.

She closed her eyes and breathed deeply, trying to pull herself together enough to finish the conversation, so she could hang up, call in sick and scream into her pillow until she fell into an exhausted sleep, the way she'd done too many times to count. Unfair.

Unfair-unfair-unfair-unfair-unfair….

"Addy."

"Yeah?"

"Have you seen the news this morning?"

She shook her head, swallowing hard a couple of times before she answered so she wouldn't sound half-strangled. "No. I don't watch the news until after dinner. It's not a positive way to start your day."

"Look—" Liz exhaled sharply into the phone "—I can't leave just now, but I'm sending someone over—"

"No." Clenching her teeth together so hard, she thought they might crack, Addy shook her head and willed herself to function. *Don't think. Don't feel.* Put James back in the little box inside her head where she kept him, so she could interact with others like a seminormal human being. Howling at them in grief never made for good conversation. "No."

"Addy, I mean it, stay there."

Grabbing a paper bag from under the sink, the phone tucked between her shoulder and chin, Addy stuffed the knife into it and headed for the door. Just before she reached it, she picked up the note from the floor and put it in the paper bag, then shoved the whole mess into her tote. "No. I'm sick of letting these idiotic pranks disrupt my life."

Liz let out a muffled groan, and Addy could visualize the exasperated, because-I'm-the-mom look on her face. "I can't tell you what's going on right now, but you really ought to stay put."

"I'm going to my car," Addy singsonged, feeling stronger now as she locked her front door. Defying Liz's prudent sense of caution always had that effect.

She made her way to the boxy little Scion XB that sat in her driveway. Fortunately, no one had yet jabbed a knife into it. "I'm getting in and turning the key. Screw you, socially stunted neighborhood children."

"Adriana, could you stop for a minute and tell me where the note is?"

Addy turned the key and put the car in gear, backing slowly out of her driveway. "Sitting next to me, along with the knife. You can send one of your lackeys to the studio to get it." Addy owned a yoga studio on Cannery Row, the trendy, store-lined street in Monterey made famous by John Steinbeck, and she had no intention of being late to her first class of the day because her neighbors were jerks. Not this time.

"Okay, look," Liz said, "I need you to pull over and read the note to me."

"Dear Miss Torres, We're coming for you. This time we mean it, just like the other seven times. Love, your friendly neighborhood troll children," Addy droned.

"You know," Liz said, her too-polite tone barely concealing her growing impatience, "you really should talk to my new partner—he's the department go-to guy for stalking cases. He could tell you some stories about why this isn't funny."

"Okay, fine." Addy sighed and fished around in her tote for the paper bag while keeping her eyes on the road. Hearing the telltale crinkle, she opened it up and picked the note out of it, unfolding it against the steering wheel. As she hit an open stretch of road, she glanced down at the contents.

Her hand involuntarily jerked the wheel; the car jolted to the right.

As the note fluttered to the car floor, Addy managed to steer the Scion to the curb, where, hands shaking, she put it in Park. She pitched forward, until her forehead rested against the steering wheel. A sickly, clammy feeling prickled across her skin, and she gripped the wheel as if it were the last thing anchoring her to the sane world. Not that. She couldn't have seen that.

"Addy?"

"Just a minute." Taking a deep, shuddering breath, she slowly raised her head and picked the note up off the floor. Instead of the childish penciled scrawls or cut-out magazine letters affixed to a page of loose-leaf that she'd received in the past, what she held was a computer printout of a photo. The image was slightly pixilated, so maybe she had been mistaken….

But then it snapped into focus. A low, soft, keening sound filled the car, and it took a moment to realize she was making it.

"Addy?" Liz snapped, the urgency in her voice carrying through the phone.

"Oh, God." Scrabbling for the driver's-side armrest, Addy punched the button to activate her automatic door locks. She twisted around to look back down her street, her pulse kicking into overdrive.

Deserted.

But who was hiding out there? Who had left this?

Who would do this to her?

Suddenly furious, she let the note fall as she smacked her hand against the window. A stinging, fiery pain shot across her palm. She curled her arm against her chest and sank back in her seat.

"Addy, for heaven's sake, tell me what the note said!"

She doubled over, trying to regain control and finding that for the first time in four years, she just couldn't. "Liz, it's awful," she gasped, trying desperately not to cry, not to lose it completely until she'd told her friend what she'd seen. "I can't breathe."

"I'm coming over."

"No. I can't go back there." Focus. She had to focus. "God, Liz, I'm afraid to go back to my own home." Pressing her palms against the steering wheel, she narrowed her focus to the space between her thumbs, inhaling through her nose, exhaling through her mouth. In. Out. In. Out. "It's different this time," she said, her voice regaining some of its former calm.

"It's James." Inhale. Detach, just like her first yoga master had taught her. *Detach. What shows up must be accepted without upset.* "It's a picture of James. Someone took a picture of his body the day he…" Exhale. Accept. She glanced at the slip of paper and the tremors in her body worsened. "Liz, I think this was taken right when he died."

Chapter Two

Adriana hugged her elbows, feeling cold and almost painfully brittle, as if someone had opened her up and exposed her insides to the world. "You don't think it's just a prank?" she said into the phone. To tell the truth, *she* didn't think it was just a prank, but something in her was holding on to that idea all the same, with the desperation of a shipwreck victim clinging to a piece of driftwood.

"No, I don't," Liz replied softly. "I was there, remember?"

The day Addy had lost James wasn't one she could easily forget. But while her experience had been confined to getting the long-dreaded visit from a cop who wasn't her fiancé, Liz's had been far more physically painful. James had been shot in the line of duty while pursuing a killer, and Liz had been right beside him when it had happened. James's murderer had taken Liz hostage for several hours, an experience she never talked about, which had landed her in the hospital for over a week. If the rumors were true, her clothes concealed some nasty knife-wound scars.

Addy looked to her right, where the ocean was barely visible between two of her neighbors' houses. She could just glimpse a tiny corner of the sharp rocks that lined their portion of the beach, around which the cold sea boiled and churned, filled with riptides ready to drag down anything that fell into it.

Elijah Carter, aka The Surgeon—the man who'd killed James, who'd nearly killed Liz—had fallen into that water, in his final confrontation with the FBI and Monterey PD. His body had never been found.

"He couldn't have survived, could he?" she asked, not taking her eyes off that sliver of blue-gray. In all the years that she'd lived on Monterey's Mermaid Point, she'd never heard of someone falling into that water, and living.

Liz didn't answer, and Addy's vision blurred, until all she could see was the mental image of James as he was in the photo lying beside her. His cheek pressed into the woodchip-lined ground, his glasses half off his face, one lens cracked in a spiderweb pattern, the rumpled brown hair she'd loved to smooth off his forehead partially obscuring his unfocused stare. He'd been breathing just seconds before that picture had been taken. She knew it. He'd been alive, and somewhere across town she'd been coming home after a day at work, engaged and in love. She'd been happy.

"Why?" The word came out broken, and sounding so lonely and scared, she wanted to take it back as soon as she'd said it.

"I don't know, Addy. I'm so sorry."

Wanting to get as far from Mermaid Point as she could, Addy said goodbye to Liz, who promised to wrap up her work at whatever scene she was at to meet her at the studio. Calling ahead to ask her office manager to cancel her classes for the day, Addy didn't stop driving until she reached the bustling street. She pulled into the little parking lot behind her studio and took the keys out of the ignition.

And then found herself unable to get out of the car.

If he survived the fall off those rocks…

The thought of leaving the Scion and walking out into the wide-open street where anyone could see her made her stomach clench. He could be anywhere. He could be watching her. She glanced at the piece of paper lying facedown on the passenger seat. Who else but the man who murdered James could have taken that photo?

The man who got off on torturing women. The man who'd stalked and nearly killed two of her friends.

She glanced at her reflection in the rearview mirror, all too aware of just how neatly she fit The Surgeon's victim profile: unmarried students or working women in their twenties and thirties, with dark hair, who live alone.

All alone.

Someone tapped on the driver's-side window, and she jerked backward in her seat. Her hand flew to her mouth to muffle her instinctive shout.

One of her students. Stan, an inexperienced yoga practitioner who'd just started coming to her beginner class a few weeks ago. Forcing a smile, which made her skin feel too tight and her jaw ache, she rolled down her window.

"Hey, Stan."

He shoved his overly long hair out of his eyes and smiled shyly at her, revealing a slight gap between his two front teeth. One of them looked slightly gray and off-kilter, as if it had been knocked out in the past and then haphazardly glued back into his mouth. "Hi, Addy."

She waited for him to let her know what he wanted, but when he remained silent—for far longer than was socially acceptable—she grabbed her bags and the stupid note and busied herself with getting out of the car. As his yoga instructor, she was probably supposed to be radiating Zenlike patience, but something about Stan had rankled from the first day he'd walked into her studio. For one thing, she'd never asked him to call her Addy—most of her students called her Adriana.

"Can I help you with something?"

"Oh, I just saw you coming, and I thought I'd wait for you." He nervously fingered the hem of his gray T-shirt, which hung a little too high over his tight bicycle shorts to be flattering. "To walk to class together, you know."

Deep breath. Maybe as Terri, the office manager, often pointed out, the more difficult students who came their way were secret bodhisattvas, put on earth to teach everyone patience. And really, Stan wasn't the worst they'd ever had—just a little socially awkward.

Slamming the door shut, she pressed the button on her key fob to lock the doors.

Twice, just in case. "I'm sorry, didn't Terri put up a sign yet? I'm having to cancel classes today."

"Ohhhh. Oh, yeah. Umm."

His stuttered reply gave her the distinct feeling that Terri had put up a sign and he'd seen it. But she pushed the thought out of her mind—she was just being paranoid. She'd read about conditions like Asperger's where people had trouble reading social cues—Stan probably deserved patience, not condemnation.

Slinging her bags over her shoulder, she started walking toward the studio, and he fell into step beside her.

"Well, um…"

"I'm really sorry," she said. "I have an emergency I'm having to deal with. We'll add a free class to your prepaid schedule to make up for it. I know how I feel when I have to miss my morning yoga." She gave a laugh that had been an attempt at being pleasant, but sounded hollow and artificial even to her ears.

"Sure, thanks, uh…"

She felt a rush of relief when they turned the corner onto Cannery Row and were suddenly playing Dodge the Tourists. Crowds. Crowds were good. Resurrected serial killers would have a hard time coming after her in a big crowd. She stopped underneath the hand-painted sign for her Laughing Lotus Yoga Studio and scanned the busy street, but she saw no evidence of Liz's car.

When she turned toward the studio, she saw that Stan had planted himself in front of the doorway, where he was simply watching her with wide, staring blue eyes.

"Do you have a question for me, Stan?" His eyes were a nice blue. A perfectly normal shade of blue with the slightest smile lines at the corners. There was nothing wrong with him—no reason for him to be setting off her alarm bells this way.

Nerves. It's just nerves.

"No—well, yes, actually, but it's not about yoga." Interrupting himself with a loud sigh, Stan rolled his eyes skyward. "Say it. Just say it. You can say it."

Her eyes flicked back to the street, and as the silence stretched between them, she willed Liz's car to appear. "Uh, Stan?"

"Would you go out with me? This Saturday, maybe? There's a great little ice cream shop in Carmel, and we could walk on the beach afterward, and I'll pick you up at one, if that's okay with you." He skimmed his hand along his hip bone during his entire nervous, rapid-fire monologue, as if trying to shove his fingers into a pocket that wasn't there. "I mean, if it's not too drizzly on the beach. It always seems to rain on the public-access parts even when the rest of the area is sunny—"

"I'm seeing someone," she blurted, cringing inwardly at the lie.

She should have known. Ever since James had died, shy, awkward men had come out from every corner of Monterey to ask her out, as if sensing that something was slightly off-kilter inside her, too. But she wasn't socially awkward—she just didn't want to socialize. She didn't want to go out on dates, she didn't want to go shopping with friends, she barely wanted to go to work in the morning. It all seemed so superficial and…unfair, since James couldn't do any of it anymore. Maybe that's why she'd upped her class load and spent more of her free time teaching, after selling the clothing boutique she used to own…before. At least teaching made her feel as if she was doing something useful with her life.

"Just as you should be," Stan murmured to the sidewalk. He shuffled his weight from side to side, his hands moving awkwardly. He really wasn't bad looking—he had a pleasant face, a healthy head of hair and a fit physique, if a little on the skinny side. But dating wasn't something she did anymore—she just couldn't drum up the energy to be attracted to someone.

"I'm sorry." She really was. And now she knew why Stan had made her uneasy—she must've known at some unconscious level that they would be having this uncomfortable conversation soon.

He nodded several times, opening his mouth once to respond and then closing it again. Still nodding, he started ambling down the street. A few seconds later, he turned around and came back to stand beside her.

"I'm sorry to put you in that position." He waved off her reflexive denial. "I don't want my being in your class to get strange. It's just…" His gaze darted across the street, and he shrugged. "My mother is in the hospital. They think she might be dying this time, and I just feel peaceful when I'm around you." He looked back at the blue-and-green sign hanging over the studio door, showing a laughing woman sitting cross-legged and holding a lotus. "I bet you have that effect on a lot of people."

She was officially a monster. The poor guy's mother was dying, and she'd been acting all uncomfortable just because he'd paid her the compliment of asking her out. "I'm so sorry, Stan. Has she been sick long?" Making a conscious effort to relax her body, she glanced down at her hands to discover she'd woven her fingers through her set of keys while they'd been talking, so a key stuck straight out between each pair—instant brass knuckles.

Stan didn't seem to notice. "Yeah. She had cancer a while back, and now it's in her lungs. They told her she has about a month left."

"I'm sorry." What do you say to something like that without resorting to clichés and stale platitudes? She couldn't even imagine going through what the poor guy was dealing with, as her own parents were strong and healthy. "Please let me know if there's anything I can do."

Instead of replying, Stan suddenly lifted his arm in the air to flag a passing taxi. With a murmured goodbye, he got inside, and the cab disappeared down the street.

A few minutes later, Liz screeched into view in her off-duty Dodge Charger, black with dark-tinted windows. Nobody loved an American muscle car better than Liz. Leaning her body against the door, Adriana curled her fingers under its handle, then stopped.

A flash of gray out of the corner of her eye. The sense that someone was staring at her.

Stan was gone—the awkward moment had passed—and yet, something still felt…off, somehow. And all she had to go on to prove it was a feeling. She watched the street, as people strolled in and out of the vibrant little shops and art galleries lining the historic street. Some paused to admire the explosions of flowers planted near curbs and on the road dividers. Many were undoubtedly headed toward the far end of the street, to either visit the famous aquarium or just for a glimpse of Monterey Bay itself. It was a pleasant scene, one straight out of the glossy, free, tourist brochures inside her studio.

And something was so wrong about it all. But what?

Still looking down the street, she opened the door and got into the car.

"SORRY I'M LATE," a deep voice said to her left, the masculine sound very unlike Liz's no-nonsense alto.

Whipping her head around in shock, she discovered that Liz wasn't inside waiting for her…and that she herself wasn't even in Liz's car. The sleek black Charger looked exactly like Liz's from the outside, but the gray interior lacked the crumpled soda cans and ballet and basketball gear her daughters perpetually left inside. Come to think of it, the familiar Truth or D.A.R.E. decal on the rear side window touting the police-run drug education program was also missing. And there was also the small detail that in the driver's seat, instead of Liz, was a man she hadn't seen in four years—one she remembered all too well.

"Lieutenant Borkowski sent me," Detective Daniel Cardenas said without preamble, which was enough to stop her from apologizing and scrambling out of the vehicle.

"You two have the same car," she replied, immediately wanting to kick herself for sounding so stupid.

"There's a Dodge dealer in town who likes cops. Nice discounts." He hit a button on the door armrest, causing all four doors to lock down with a loud thud. "Buckle up."

She clicked her seat belt into place, knowing that if Liz had sent him, she'd had a good reason for doing so. "So, Detective, you want to tell me why Liz isn't picking me up herself like she promised?"

"She said she promised you a ride, Ms. Torres," he said, as unfailingly polite as she remembered. Despite the Latin last name—he was Puerto Rican, she remembered—his English was unaccented, until he said her name with the rolling *R* and musical tone of a native Spanish speaker.

"Adriana. Or Addy," she said. He didn't invite her to call him Daniel—and she knew he wouldn't. If Cardenas was going to have anything to do with her case, he would keep things professional.

Concentrating intently on the road, he pulled the car away from the curb. He didn't smile—she couldn't remember ever having seen him smile—but his face was relaxed, pleasant. "She thought we should talk."

"Oh?" Obviously, getting information out of Mr. Strong and Silent was going to be about as easy as bathing Liz's cat. When Cardenas didn't offer any further information, Adriana sat back in her seat, seeing if waiting patiently would produce some results.

Four years ago, at the age of twenty-eight, Daniel Cardenas had become the youngest detective sergeant in the City of Monterey Police Department's history, James had told her. Known for his sharpshooting skills and a constant, almost preternatural cool under pressure that had earned him the nickname

"The Zen Master," the quiet detective with a rumored genius-level IQ had a case-solve rate that rivaled the best in the department, including Liz and James.

At one of the police department's social events, Cardenas's date had confided to Adriana that she referred to him as "The Kama Sutra Master" with her girlfriends, because "he had really great hands." Fortunately, Addy had managed to excuse herself before the woman had provided any more details.

He was now dressed in a blue-gray silk tie and a tailored white shirt with the sleeves rolled up. His dark gray suit jacket lay abandoned in the backseat, a fact that made her realize she'd never seen him look that rumpled. He'd always been buttoned up, pressed and coolly professional, usually with a pair of mirrored aviators hiding his dark eyes and making him look like Secret Service. Even his short, black hair was cool, the cut a combination of artfully mussed style and low-maintenance casualness that you couldn't get from a discount barber.

She glanced at his hands, loosely clamped around the steering wheel at three and nine o'clock, the tendons standing out in sharp relief underneath his tanned skin. No rings.

She remembered those hands. They'd held her for hours after he'd come to her door to tell her that James had died in the line of duty. They'd wiped her tears and had dialed the phone to call her family. They'd stroked her hair and had given her something to hold on to when she thought she'd die because it hurt so much.

Seeing him again was like a handsome, polite reminder of the worst day of her life.

The car crawled slowly through the tourists on Cannery Row, and since Cardenas seemed more focused on his driving than on enlightening her, she decided to start playing twenty questions. "You're the one she was telling me about?" she asked, more than a little glad her voice sounded more normal than she felt. "The MPD 'go-to guy' on stalking cases?"

A corner of his mouth quirked upward. It wasn't quite a smile, but it was closer than she'd ever seen. Not that they'd crossed paths all that often. "Something like that."

"But this might be more than just a stalking case."

He nodded, a small, economic movement, quickly glancing in the rearview mirror before responding further. "I know."

She turned her face away from him to stare out the window.

Arriving at the Hoffman Avenue intersection in time for a break in the tourists meandering through the crosswalks, Daniel made a sudden left. He followed that with an immediate, sharp right onto Lighthouse that had her grasping for the armrest so she wouldn't careen into his side. She could have sworn she heard the tires squealing.

As she peeled herself off the door, she noticed he was driving calmly, as if the two Indy 500 turns he'd just made had never happened.

"Uh, Detective," she said. "Is there something you need to tell me?"

"I like to drive fast."

Okay, now he was just messing with her. And she was about to let him have it when everything clicked into place—the off-duty car, the rolled-up sleeves, the slightly askew tie.

"This isn't official is it? You're off duty."

"I'm never off duty," he replied, extremely focused on the road. "But I'm officially on the clock in exactly two minutes, if it makes you feel better."

"Look. I don't know what Liz told you, but I don't need to waste the department's time—

and yours, since you're not even on the clock at the moment, and I know they just cut the overtime budget because Liz has been ranting about that for weeks."

Another glance in his mirrors. He slipped a pair of expensive aviators out of his shirt pocket and put them on, hiding his eyes. "You're not wasting my time, Adriana."

The rolling R again. She was a native Spanish speaker, and his accent still sounded sexy to her. "I am. I'm not rich or important enough to pull police off the streets—or out of their homes—for my personal protection. We're not sure that The Surgeon is still alive. Frankly, I don't see how he could be." *Liar.* "Take me back to work, Detective, and then go do whatever it is you need to do for the day." She just wanted to get out of the car, away from the hot guy with communication problems. Away from the memories he'd brought with him.

"Adriana Maria Imaculata Torres, age thirty-six," he said, calmly staring at the road. "Parents are Ana Maria and Juan Roberto Torres of Carmel, net worth approximately $1.6 billion, mostly from the sale of the Asilomar Tire Company they inherited in 1972, which had been in the family for approximately three generations. Today the family owns a small vineyard that boasts several award-winning chardonnays and a tragically underrated merlot."

Adriana could only stare at him.

"You are that rich, according to the *Monterey County Herald,*" he supplied, making a puzzling series of right turns that had them going pretty much in a circle through downtown. "And everyone's important enough to make their safety paramount."

Safety *paramount?* Who talked like that?

"Detective?"

"Hmm?" They'd hit Asilomar, one of the busier roads. Cardenas glanced in his mirrors and accelerated past two cars that had been meandering along.

"How about we not mention my middle name ever again, please? No one should ever saddle their child with something as horrible as Imaculata, even though it was my great-grandmother's name, God rest her soul."

The almost smile appeared again. "Catholic family?"

"You know it." She didn't know why, but it had suddenly become her challenge in life to make him smile outright, or maybe even laugh. Maybe because it kept her from thinking too hard about why Liz was so afraid for her safety, she'd pulled a hardworking detective off of his undoubtedly heavy caseload to babysit her. "Do you really think The Surgeon might be back?"

"I know you're not asking for my advice, but call him Carter. It'll remind you that he was just a man."

A man who liked to carve people up for fun.

"Let me ask you a question," Daniel said gently when she didn't respond. "Is there anyone else it could be?"

Her hands flew briefly into the air, palms upward. "I don't know. I'm pretty sure at least some of the notes I've gotten over the years have been from some teenagers who live near me. I even got a glimpse of one once, and he was definitely just shy of puberty. But this…it seemed different."

"Let's assume it is different," he replied. Darn those glasses. She couldn't see his eyes, and without that, she didn't have a prayer of reading his expression. "Who else might want to upset you?"

She had to think about that one. Truthfully, she tried to avoid conflict and didn't have any enemies she could think of. "Well, there's…" She let the sentence trail off.

"There's who?" he prompted gently.

"It's nothing." She shrugged. "Just a stupid thought."

"Coworker? Customer? Some guy who passes you on the street every day and acts a little strange?"

"I was going to say there's this guy in one of my yoga classes—a student. But he's harmless, really. Just because someone is a little socially awkward—"

He took the glasses off and tossed them on the dash. "Adriana, I'd really like it if you'd give me permission to come into your house when I drop you off. There are a couple of things I haven't told you yet." He flicked a glance at her, and though she'd known his eyes were hazel, she hadn't noticed the almost hypnotic combination of green and gold, until that split second. And then she remembered—when Daniel Cardenas looked at you, even for just a moment, he really looked at you. And he must have known the effect he had when he did, or he wouldn't have removed those damned sunglasses just then.

She didn't want to deal with his pity. She didn't want to show him her drab house and the refrigerator that lacked all the things you offered a guest. She didn't want him to have to keep up that unfailing politeness while he witnessed how sad and pathetic her life had become.

But someone was out there. Taking pictures of the dead.

And so she had to know what his last sentence had meant. "What things?"

"I can't tell you how many times a victim I've interviewed has said, 'I was going to mention this guy as a possible suspect, but he's harmless,' and the guy turned out to be not so harmless." He glanced in the rearview mirror. He'd been doing that a lot, so she looked over her shoulder, too, but all she saw were a couple of innocuous cars cruising along behind them.

She waited for his second point, but instead he just asked, "See that handle up there?"

She blinked at the odd non sequitur. "What?"

"The grab handle." He motioned slightly with his chin toward the interior handle near the roof. She'd always thought those were put there to hold dry cleaning.

"Yes."

"Hang on to it."

As soon as her fingers curled around it, Daniel calmly put the gear shift in Neutral. Then, he cranked the steering wheel to the left, yanking up hard on the emergency brake. With an ear-splitting squeal of its tires, the Charger spun in a tight half circle, fast and hard. Her right side slammed into the passenger door. "What are you—"

But Daniel wasn't in the mood for questions. His mouth set in a grim line, he let down the brake handle and punched the accelerator, probably leaving most of his tire treads on the asphalt as the car shot forward. The force of it slammed Addy back in her seat. They zoomed past the cars that had been behind them. So fast, Addy couldn't get even a glimpse of the drivers. As soon as they hit an intersection, Daniel took another hairpin turn to the right. He followed that with a tire-squealing left through a traffic light that had just changed from yellow to red.

After one more careening left turn, Daniel finally slowed down to an acceptable speed, leaving Addy reeling in her seat, dizzy and more than a little car sick.

"Do you always drive like this?" she asked, tentatively loosening her death grip on the grab handle. "Because if you do, I'm so going to throw up on you."

The half smile actually turned into a full-fledged grin, a flash of straight, white teeth that contrasted against his brown skin.

"You're laughing at me." She fussed with the hoodie sweatshirt she'd tied around her waist to make her black, flared-leg spandex pants a little more modest as streetwear.

"I don't laugh at crime victims." His expression turned serious once more. He had a nice smile, and despite her confusion over what had just happened and the fear that had been lingering on the edge of her conscience all day, she kind of wished it had stayed a little longer.

"What just happened there? Because I think it was more than a boys-and-their-toys moment."

Signaling a turn for the first time since she'd gotten into the car with him, he pulled the Charger onto Mermaid Point Drive. He parked the car in front of her little clapboard house.

"You know that guy who walked out of your store with you? Left in a taxi?"

"Stan?" But Cardenas hadn't even pulled up until several minutes *after* Stan had left.

"He had the cab circle back and then got out on a side street," he said. "He was watching you when I picked you up, and then he got into a blue Ford Taurus."

Oh, no. "But why would he get in a cab if—"

"I lost him on that side street back there,

or he probably would have followed us all the way to your house." Those green-and-gold eyes were back on her, radiating an intensity that made her want to squirm in her seat. "Still think he's harmless?"

Chapter Three

Though even under torture Daniel Cardenas wouldn't have shown it, coming face-to-face with Adriana Torres for the first time in four years felt something like the time a bank robber had hit him with a stun gun.

He'd come to Cannery Row looking for her, so the fact that she'd gotten into the car wasn't the shock of the century. It was her face, or more accurately, her expression, the way she walked, the way she moved, as if she was constantly trying to fold into herself. He'd known her for nearly a decade, and although they'd been no more than casual acquaintances, he'd never seen her look so…subdued.

Then again, he shouldn't have been surprised. He knew what she'd been through. Violence changed you, especially when it happened to someone you loved.

Beautiful girl. I wish we could have saved him.

He got out of the car and walked around it to open her door. She ignored his outstretched hand.

"Liz said you have a wireless Internet connection," he told her as she unfolded her tall, slender frame from the car. He reached into the backseat, pulling out his laptop case. "If you don't mind my connecting to it, I'll tell you everything you should know."

When Liz had called him aside as they'd gotten back to the station after processing last night's crime scene to ask him a favor, he'd said yes before she'd even had time to explain what she wanted. Because that's what you did when a fellow cop needed you. That's what you did when your partner needed you.

And when she'd told him that Elijah Carter, if he were indeed still alive, might decide to target the late Detective Brentwood's fiancée, he'd shuffled his caseload for the next month to make Adriana a priority. He'd even offered to cancel his diving trip to the Caymans, which was supposed to start tomorrow. You never turned your back on a fallen cop's family. But Liz had insisted he go.

He followed her up the small pathway flanked by flowers and a couple of shrubs that were so overgrown an army of burglars could hide in them. She unlocked the door, which had both a door lock and a dead bolt—good. And then they were inside.

He remembered when he'd been there last time. Adriana was an amateur artist, and the whole place had been decorated with vibrant oil paintings, photographs and objects encrusted in stained-glass mosaic tiles. Now it felt as if someone had come along and sucked most of the color out of the room—all of her pieces were gone, save one coffee table with a mosaic top made of broken china. The majority of the room's surfaces were now bare—those that weren't held candles or photographs of Adriana with James Brentwood. Her home had become as dark and drab as the black clothes she wore.

Though he'd known her for a long time, he hadn't known her well. But funny thing—he still missed the color.

Adriana gestured for him to sit on the pale-green couch, as she pulled a fluffy gray throw off its cushions and hurriedly folded it. Gathering up a couple of mugs that sat on the coffee table, she hustled them into the kitchen, then hustled back and sat down in the chair across from him. She leaned forward to swat at some dust he couldn't see on the coffee table, then finally relaxed.

"Sorry about the mess," she said. "I didn't realize I was going to have company. I mean, other than Liz who is used to my chaos."

"'S'okay," he replied. "We just need someplace quiet to talk." Leaning toward her, he rested his elbows on his knees. "Liz wanted me to advise you on the best ways to protect yourself, and how the MPD can help."

Her only answer was to grab a dark throw pillow and hug it to her chest.

He pulled his laptop out of its case and set it on the table, firing it up on battery power. "Like you said earlier, I'm the one who handles most of the stalking cases we get, which isn't quite the situation we have going on here, but it translates. I was also on the task force handling Elijah Carter's case—"

"I remember," she said, a faraway look in her eyes. "You came here. The day James—"

"Yeah." He cut her off before she could say *died* and go into what else lay unspoken between them, including the fact that he'd been the one to tell her that her fiancé had been killed. It was his face she imagined when she thought about the worst day of her life. His arms that had wrapped around her for comfort when they should have been James Brentwood's.

It never got easier, telling people they'd lost someone. They knew as soon as they saw a cop coming to their door that the news would be the worst kind. Some of them dropped to the ground in hysterics, wailing before you could say a word. Some of them cried silently, tears streaming down their faces until you'd finished your piece, and then they couldn't slam the door on you soon enough. Some argued with you, somehow convinced that they could undo the truth by making you take back your words. And some bolted, figuring if they could outrun you, they could outrun the news you'd brought.

Adriana's reaction haunted him more than any other, maybe because it had been connected to the premature death of his own friend and colleague. Or maybe because he'd seen her through the years at department gatherings, and he'd known what she'd been like when she'd been happy.

Her pretty face had crumpled before she'd collapsed into a chair, and then she'd just reached her arms out, as if James would come any second to hold her. Of course, he hadn't. And Daniel had been a damn poor substitute, under the circumstances.

He remembered the way her tears had soaked through the fabric of his jacket, and the frustrated helplessness he'd felt. More than any other house call, except the ones that were about children, he wished then that he could have made the news of her boyfriend's death untrue.

He remembered the curve of her neck, and the way her hair smelled like spices. He remembered not wanting to let her go and then mentally kicking his own ass for even going there.

He remembered wanting to keep her safe. He still wanted to keep her safe.

"I never thanked you…then. You stayed with me for so long." Picking up yet another picture of herself and James from the coffee table, she traced her finger around the wooden frame. "That must have been so awful for you."

He looked away, jabbing at the space bar as if it would make his computer boot up faster. "You did say thank you. I was just doing my job."

"You did more than your job, Detective."

Adriana put the photograph down and shifted her focus to him.

She should have looked scared, but instead she just seemed tired. And not at all like the vibrant free spirit he'd seen on James's arm during their shared years on the force.

Every time he'd noticed her at a department function or when she'd drop by the station to see James, she'd wrapped herself in blazing, bright colors and wild patterns. All the better to advertise the stuff she sold at the Trashy Diva, her used-clothing store, James had once explained. But she'd sold the store, he'd heard, and at Brentwood's funeral she'd worn black.

Four years later, she was still wearing black—black sweatshirt tied around the waist of her black exercise pants, the whole outfit finished off with a black tank that hugged her flat stomach and a waist he could have spanned with his hands. The only color in her clothing choices was the bit of silver embroidery on her black flip-flops.

And the short hair that had shown off her Hepburnlike neck had grown out past her shoulders, still pretty, but he could tell it hadn't been cut in a long time. She'd stopped highlighting it with red streaks, too, so it had gone back to its natural dark brown color. A few delicate lines had formed around her eyes, but otherwise she still looked the same. Still herself but…muted.

He fought the urge to scrub a hand down his face. Part of the job was the facade of looking cool and completely in control at all times, down to avoiding nervous twitches. He had to make a victim trust him, make her believe that his sole focus was her well-being. Because that trust could mean the difference between life and death, if things went south.

"You said back in the car that Stan had doubled back and was watching me," she said when he asked her about Stan. "How did you know?" She shifted in her seat, her hands on the armrests as if she'd spring up and dart out the door the first chance she got.

"I cruised by your studio before you got there and saw him pacing in front of the door. Ran him in on a petty theft charge a few years back." Reaching back into the laptop briefcase at his feet, he pulled out a file and opened it up, taking a sheet of paper out. "He got off on a plea bargain—turned out he'd been rolling with a crowd connected to a drug lord the vice squad had been watching for a while. We got him to squeal in exchange for a fine and no jail time."

Her eyes were a light brown, the color of polished chunks of amber or really good scotch, and they widened to the point where the irises were rimmed with white. "Stan has a police record?"

"Not a long one. Just that and—" he flipped through the papers in the file "—a restraining order from an ex-girlfriend in Gilroy. Seems old Stanley Robert Peterson had a hard time saying goodbye. Has he expressed any romantic interest in you?"

"Yes. Just today, he...asked me out. He didn't get upset or violent when I turned him down. He just looked a little sad." She shook her head, her eyebrows drawing together in confusion. "He seems harmless."

"His ex-girlfriend doesn't think so. The Gilroy detective I talked to says he threw a chair at her during an argument they had."

"Stan? Seriously?" She pulled her legs up onto the seat and wrapped her arms around them. "Well, maybe he was upset because his mom was dying."

"Who told you that?" Daniel asked.

"Stan did." She did not like where this was going.

Daniel leaned forward, his face sober. "His mom lives in Salinas. She works in housekeeping at at local hotel."

Unbelievable. He'd lied to her.

"So you saw him and went back out to watch him?"

"Pretty much."

She remained silent, which he was starting to realize meant she was waiting for more information. "I followed his taxi," he continued. "He had the cab circle around and then got out about a block away from you. He ducked into a recessed doorway and watched you, until I picked you up. At that point, he got into a blue Taurus and followed us until I lost him."

"But why?"

"You're a beautiful woman," he said matter-of-factly. "Looks like he's formed an attachment."

She abruptly broke eye contact at the compliment, becoming preoccupied with twisting a slim sapphire-and-gold ring on her right hand.

He hadn't been flirting, but judging from her reaction to what had just come shooting out of his mouth, she would have shut him down big-time if he had been. "Liz said you'd gotten a note?"

She nodded, looking relieved that he'd changed the subject, and left the room. He heard a crinkling sound, and then she returned carrying a small paper bag, which she silently handed to him. He extracted the folded piece of paper inside, then looked in at the knife that had accompanied it.

Serrated edge, about twelve inches long, made for hunting. There were several just like it still in Evidence downtown.

He *really* didn't like where this was going.

"You get one of these knives before?"

"No," she answered. "I've gotten knives, but they tend to be the cheap butcher kind."

Interesting. He rolled the bag shut and set it carefully on the table. Then he unfolded the note.

Liz had told him what that piece of paper contained, but nothing prepared him for the emotional sucker punch to the gut it delivered in reality.

James Brentwood, waxy looking and still. Just as he'd been in his last moments on earth, before the M.E. had shown up to collect "the body." Before a team of Monterey PD had carried him to his grave and put one of their own in the ground. His mentor. His friend. Adriana's almost husband.

It could have been Daniel. Maybe it should have been.

He stole a glance at Adriana, who hugged a pillow to her chest and was overly absorbed in picking at the fabric, her long legs tucked underneath her as she folded into herself once more. He didn't have anyone who would have grieved for him the way she still did for James.

Damn Elijah Carter to hell.

She looked up suddenly and met his gaze head-on. "You're quiet." There was something almost accusatory in the way she said it.

"This must have been terrifying for you." He folded the note again and put it back into the paper bag.

"It was but…" Her dark eyebrows drew together, and a slim line appeared in between them. "He worked with you, Detective. You saw him, talked with him every day—probably more than I did, he was such a workaholic." She released her stranglehold on the pillow, her hands making empty gestures in the air. "And I just… You just…*sit* here, looking at that awful picture, and…"

"Adriana," he said softly. "Would it really do you any good if I started cursing or throwing things?"

She froze and just stared at him.

"Because I could. No problem." A corner of his mouth quirked upward in a wry smile that he knew held no trace of mirth. "I'm not exactly getting paid to sit in your living room and emote, though."

A lone tear slipped down her cheek, and before he realized what he was doing, he'd reached out and brushed it away with one finger.

"I'm sorry," she whispered.

His hand lingered against her skin, and suddenly it was as if they were the only two people in the world, and all he could look at was her.

"Don't be," he replied. "I'm sorry he didn't come home to you that night."

She jerked back, and the moment between them was gone. Who knew if it had really existed, or if it was just his overworked imagination and the fact that he'd been too damn tired to go on a date since the city government had slashed the police department budget last spring.

He sat back in his chair, all business again. "James was a hell of a cop. And he taught me more than anyone else on the force. I miss him every day. We all do."

She bit her lower lip. "So, in the picture, was it taken when—"

"Yes," he said, wanting to keep her from having to finish her sentence. "It was." Something had been nagging at him about that photo, but he couldn't put his finger on what it was.

She didn't speak for a moment, and then she just started talking, telling him about all of the other notes she'd gotten over the years—seven in total, and always around the anniversary of James's death. He questioned her about what she'd seen each time she found a note, about her daily routine. And the information just came pouring out, as if she'd kept all the details and the emotions surrounding them bottled up for too long.

"Do you think Stan could have left that note?" she asked. "And if so, how could he have gotten that picture of James?"

He shook his head. He hated telling her he wasn't sure, but he wasn't going to lie. "I don't know. It's an interesting coincidence that the photo was delivered the same day he decided to declare his affections, but—" he closed the manila file and tossed it onto the table "—we don't have any evidence connecting him to James's death or the threats you've gotten. Yet."

"Other than that one argument with his ex, there's nothing else in his record? No violence?"

"No."

"Do you think there's a chance that he's not connected to the notes, that the picture had nothing to do with him?"

"Yes."

She snapped to attention at his quick response, her gaze clear and direct. "So do you think The Surg—uh, Elijah Carter might have…survived? That he's back?"

Hell, yes, he did. He had to, because even the slimmest chance meant someone would die unless the Monterey PD was prepared to meet him head-on, locked and loaded.

He didn't want to terrify Adriana, but he needed her to understand just what kind of danger she could be in.

"With the right gun, James Brentwood could hit a target from five football fields away, and sometimes the wrong gun." She flinched when he said James's name, but he forced himself to go on. "He could immobilize an armed victim with his bare hands. He had a sixth sense about danger that all of us who worked with him envied. If anyone could have gotten away from Elijah Carter, it would have been James."

He stood, and walked around the coffee table to her chair. She didn't look up at him, so he spoke to the top of her head. "Yes, there's a chance. I think you need to put something between you and him if he is alive. Because if Carter sent that threat, then he's definitely targeting you. Stalking and terrifying his victims before he attacked them was part of his signature."

He crouched down in front of her, reaching out for her hand before he realized what he was doing. But he didn't touch her. "I know this has got to be hell for you, going through this again, but...there's something I haven't told you." In the barest and briefest way possible, he gave her the slimmest, need-to-know details of the Janie Sanchez murder. "The MO was almost exactly like Elijah Carter's, although there may be some significant differences. I need to get the medical examiner's report before I'm sure."

Wrapping her arms around her middle, she hugged herself and shut her eyes briefly, then opened them once more. "Carter died, Detective. The police told us he died in the ocean. *You* told me he died."

"We never found the body."

"But you said the police and the FBI had been on the beach for hours after he fell into the water. How could he have survived that fall—which nearly no one survives—and not resurface where someone could see him?"

"It was dark. The way you survive a riptide is you let it sweep you out as far as it needs to, and then you swim parallel to shore until you reach calmer water and can swim back." He moved back to his seat. "He could have evaded us, but it's not likely. There's a possibility, that's all."

"So then, who killed Janie Sanchez if it wasn't Carter?"

"Could be a copycat. Carter and his victims got a lot of publicity once the case closed. It's not hard to find all the details."

"What about Stan?"

He had to admit, nothing fit. Stan, the note, last night's murder victim, Elijah Carter. All pieces of an intricate puzzle that right now seemed to hinge on a dead man coming back to life. "We're picking up Stan for questioning. We might not be able to arrest him for anything, but he's a person of interest at the moment."

She threw down the pillow she'd been holding all this time and sat forward. "Right. So you're telling me you don't know. Could be Stan, could be The Surgeon. Could be someone else entirely, and Stan's just coincidentally started following me around town. Could be anyone. Could be you."

She looked up at him then, and another tear slipped down her cheek. She swiped at it with the back of her hand, obviously trying hard to keep herself under control.

Without thinking, he moved forward a little. And then somehow, against his better judgment, against all rules of professionalism, they ended up reaching for each other, and she crumpled into his arms.

"I'm sorry," she said hoarsely, still trying mightily to stifle her emotions. Instead of crying, she started to tremble, and he gripped her tighter, as if he could hold back her fear, as if he could stop what was coming just by touching her.

"Don't," he said gruffly. He didn't know what to do with himself, so he just held on, rubbing her back with his palm and feeling grateful that one of his colleagues couldn't come in and find him acting like a hormonal teenager who couldn't keep his hands off a civilian.

Several minutes later, when she finally stopped shaking, she loosened her grip around his neck and pulled away. She never did give in to the flood of tears he'd expected—not that he would have blamed her one bit if she had cried.

He missed her warmth, her softness, almost immediately, but he stood up, put his hands behind his back.

Looking very uncomfortable, she picked at one of her cuticles. "I'm sorry. I just— It's all so—"

"It's okay, Adriana," he said softly. "I'd lose it if I'd been through everything you have."

That got a little smile out of her. "You wouldn't."

"Sure. I cry all the time."

She almost laughed at that one. "Yes, I bet all of you big, bad detectives cry a lot. You probably sit around and have talking circles and therapeutic group hugs every week."

"Something like that."

Steepling her hands in front of her full, pretty mouth, she inhaled deeply. "I seem to fall apart on you whenever we meet."

"All in a day's work, ma'am," he deadpanned.

"Thank you, Detective." Then the shadow of a smile was gone, her face serious once more. "You know, you've given me all the possible scenarios, but what do *you* think? About whether The Surgeon could be behind this? James always used to tell me that there was nothing more trustworthy than a good cop's instinct."

"There's something else I have to show you."

If it were any other person, he'd just tell her. But somehow, where Adriana Torres was concerned, he just wanted to protect her. And that included having to bat down the instinctive desire to keep the most disturbing information from her. But she was an intelligent woman, and she was strong as hell, too. She not only could handle what he had to tell her, but she needed to know—her safety depended on her knowing exactly what the threat was at all times.

"Elijah Carter liked computers. Frequented hacker chat rooms, broke into his victims' accounts to track their movements." He went back to his seat and sat down, leaning forward to tap a few keys on his laptop keyboard. He called up the screen he wanted. "When I was at the Sanchez scene this morning, I woke up one of our computer-crimes people and asked him to start searching for any sign that Carter might be back." Beckoning her closer, he tilted the monitor to give her a better view of what he'd called up. "I have to warn you, this is going to be disturbing."

It was a Web site. With pictures of her plastered all over it, in poses ranging from provocative to pornographic. Every photo on the screen had gaping black holes in place of her eyes.

At first she barely reacted to the images, probably because they were too bizarre, too shocking for her to comprehend.

"That isn't me," she said carefully, rising out of her seat and coming forward to examine the screen. "I've never worn those clothes, or posed…like that."

"They've been manipulated," he said softly. "If you look carefully enough, you can see where your face was digitally pasted on someone else's body, but I had our expert confirm it." Whoever had altered the pictures had done it well; her face blended seamlessly with the bodies of other women in crude poses. Even the black holes replacing her eyes looked real.

And then Adriana's face drained of color, her breathing growing more ragged as the intent behind the photos finally hit her:

Someone was fantasizing about doing those things to her, posing her in that way. Someone was thinking about gouging out her eyes.

Chapter Four

Oh, God. OhGod-ohGod-ohGod-ohGod.

This was so much worse than she'd ever imagined, ever let herself imagine. A couple of years back, she'd thought she'd gotten a glimpse of a teenager leaving one of the notes at her door, and since then, she'd been content to dismiss them all as teenage pranks. But this, on the Internet? This was too real.

The Surgeon had been good with computers. The Surgeon had hacked into some of his victims' accounts.

The Surgeon had painstakingly, meticulously stalked his victims, until he'd caught them at home or walking the streets alone in the dark. And then…

The first picture looked real. It had been taken when Adriana had been walking on the beach. Her face, her body, fully clothed in an outfit that hung in her closet. But her eyes had been convincingly blacked out by a computer program that had replaced them with dark hollows.

Written underneath: "Trembling hands reach out to stop me, she vomits lies she's learned by rote."

In the second picture the camera had caught her staring unfocused into the distance, giving her a slightly glassy-eyed look. Her head had been digitally connected to someone else's naked body, tied spread-eagle to a bed with a filthy, bare mattress. A floating knife sliced across her neck every few seconds, each time accompanied by a shrilly digital scream programmed into the site.

The caption under that read: "And I whisper that I love her with my knife held to her throat."

"Can you turn the volume off?" she asked, unable to take her eyes off the screen.

Daniel quickly complied. "Sure. Sorry."

Reaching around him, she put a finger on the touchpad and scrolled down the screen. Her arm was just shy of touching him, brushing ever so slightly against his rolled-up shirtsleeves as she moved.

He moved over to give her more room. "Do you want to sit down?"

She didn't respond. Couldn't.

The third photo showed her with her eyes wide-open and bloodshot. Her complexion had been altered so it matched the grayish tinge of the body to which it had been digitally attached, and her lips had been colored blue. The body—not hers—was smeared in blood, and the stomach was so carved up, it looked like something out of a horror film. Not real. Please let it not be real.

Dozens of other cuts marred the skin, long slices that gaped open in bloody ovals across her legs, along her arms, between her breasts.

She pulled her hand off the mouse as if it had caught fire and she stumbled backward, her own stomach heaving in response to what she'd just seen.

This was a crime-scene photo. With her face on it.

"Turn it off." Gasping for air, she spun around and braced her hands on the back of her living-room sofa, digging her nails into the soft sage-green velvet.

"Adriana—"

Breathe. Just breathe. The last thing the detective probably needed was to deal with her version of female helplessness. She had a red belt in hapkido. She knew how to use a stun gun. Her cell phone and the remote key fob that activated her security system rarely left her side. She was anything but helpless.

When she turned around, Daniel was right there, in her space, and, tall as she was, it was his collarbone that was at her eye level, not his face.

Once upon a time he'd wrapped his arms around her and had held her against that broad chest, on the worst day of her life. And if she just reached out, just a little bit, maybe she could lean against him again….

"Adriana."

Staying where she was, she tilted her head and looked up, into a pair of green-and-gold eyes. She could read them now—they were filled with concern.

He leaned toward her, his hand lifting to skim her bare arm, sending goose bumps tracking across her skin.

Goose bumps. She broke eye contact to look at the prickled skin on her arms. No one had given her goose bumps since… She stumbled guiltily back, away from him, away from his concern and his too-sexy eyes.

He cleared his throat, taking a step back himself. "Is there someone I could call?"

Stay with me.

Squeezing her hands into tight fists at her sides, her nails jabbing into her palms, she promised herself she wouldn't say it, wouldn't get all needy and clingy. He was overworked as it was….

Overworked.

He'd been up since the early morning at the Sanchez crime scene. He should be at work now, not wasting time with her, now that he'd done his duty and had told her to keep watchful.

"Do you need to go? I mean, I'm sure the Sanchez family needs you more than I do right now."

His expression softened even more, and for a minute, she was again transported back to the day when he came to her door with news no woman should ever have to hear. "I'm a cop. We take care of our own."

Our own. He was here, going above and beyond the call of duty, because she was James Brentwood's fiancée.

Remember that. Remember before you catch his arm and beg him not to leave.

He was still standing so close.

The doorbell chimed, and it was enough to keep her from reaching for him. Instead she sidestepped away from him and dug her hand into the bag she'd carelessly tossed on the sofa. Pulling out her keys, she held up the remote keychain that, with the touch of a button, would activate her security system.

"See? Touch this button, and someone's calling the cops in forty-five seconds or less," she quoted her security company's promise, always repeated in its TV and radio advertising. "I'll be fine. I know how strapped the department budget is. You can't afford to have an on-duty detective babysitting me."

"Right. Well..." He tugged at his collar. A nervous gesture—something she rarely saw him perform. "Just so you know, I've called someone to keep watch over your house today and this evening, in case I get tied up with Stan. A friend in the security business who owes me a favor. He's a good guy. You can trust him."

She started to protest, but he raised a hand, his fingers hovering over but not touching her lips. "Please, Adriana. It's either that or Liz will insist on spending the night here, away from her kids."

Well, when he put it like that...

He pulled a slim cell phone out of his jacket pocket. "We've got an all-points bulletin out for Stan, to bring him in for questioning. I'll let you know if we get anything out of him tonight."

"Okay, great. Thank you." Her voice sounded too high pitched. Too cheerful. Almost singsongy.

"Look, Addy, I could—"

"Go." Placing her hands on his shoulders, she gently steered him toward the door, allowing her palms to linger for just a moment on the flat expanse of his well-muscled back, the fabric of his suit rough under her touch. "You've done enough."

They walked to her front door, in silence, and just as he was about to pull it open, he turned back around to face her.

He'd called her Addy.

He looked at her for a long time, something deep and unspoken and unfinished sitting between them, like a heavy weight she couldn't name.

"I left my card on your coffee table," he finally said. "Call me if you need anything. I could—"

"Take care," she replied.

Stay with me.

But of course, he didn't. Because she didn't ask him to.

THE REST OF THE DAY passed rather uneventfully. Daniel introduced her to his friend

Jason, a self-described "freelance security specialist" with a military high-and-tight haircut and a penchant for dropping the fact that he was a retired Marine. "Spec ops—could tell you what I did, but then I'd have to make you disappear. Heh." She'd invited Jason inside, but he'd insisted on remaining across the street in a shiny black SUV that looked as if it would have been right at home in the presidential motorcade. Every hour or so he'd come in to check on her and use the bathroom, and she'd send him outside with a caffeinated beverage and whatever snacks she could scrounge up.

Daniel called midafternoon to let her know that Stan had "disappeared," asking her to call him right away if he attempted to contact her.

Normally, she liked being at home. With a good book and her beautiful view of the ocean, there wasn't a whole lot else that she needed. But since Daniel and Jason had highly recommended that she lie low for a while—preferably by staying inside—it had the perverse effect of making her itch to go outside. And as the day wore on, that itch just kept getting worse.

Sure, Elijah Carter liked to stalk his victims, until he finally caught them unaware and moved in for the kill. Creepy notes, like the one she'd received that morning, and phone calls were his specialty. And a young woman had just been found murdered in his macabre, signature style. With all that in mind, she should be glad to have Jason sitting outside her door and Daniel and Liz checking in by phone every so often.

For the millionth time that day she sat down at the small computer table tucked into a corner of her living room, halfheartedly checking her e-mail and surfing a few book-related sites to see if anything good had been published in the two hours since she'd last checked.

With a loud click, the power suddenly went out. Her computer screen unceremoniously flashed at her, then went blank. She hadn't realized that the sky had grown completely dark. Now that the power was out, the only light she had was coming from the streetlight outside her window, sending a stream of brightness through her gauzy blue curtains.

"Nice." Random power outages weren't uncommon in Monterey, or in California in general. But when she looked outside, she noticed the lights in her neighbors' windows were still fully visible through the thin curtains.

That was not right.

A loud thump made her start, and then she heard something being dragged along her home's exterior south wall.

Jason. It's just Jason. He would have seen all the lights go off, so no doubt he was checking around outside to see if anything was amiss. He'd probably be knocking on her door any minute.

A shadow darted past her window. Instinctively, she backed into one of the room's darker corners. She remained frozen there for several moments, blood rushing in her ears and her skin prickling with cold, irrational fear.

Jason. It's just Jason.

But why wouldn't he have talked to her first, instead of skulking around and creeping her out even more? She really was going to have to have a word with him when he did finally come inside.

It took an enormous effort to move toward the window, when all she really wanted to do was bolt for the back of the house and lock herself in her bedroom.

But then she'd be cornered, without a way out.

So she moved forward, step by step, until the window was close enough to touch. Slowly slipping her fingers around the edge of the curtain, her heart pounding like a fist inside her rib cage, she pulled the thin fabric back from the glass. Just a bit, just so she could see…

Nothing. The street in front of her home was deserted. Jason's black SUV sat in the same spot across the street where it had been all day.

But the driver's-side door had been flung open. The interior light was on. And unless Jason was lying down on the floor of his vehicle, he wasn't inside—or anywhere near it.

That's because he was prowling around her house, making creepy thumping noises and scaring her to death. Of course.

The hollow, almost musical sound of something tapping on glass rang out from the back of the house. She whirled around, staring at the black hollow of a doorway through which her kitchen and dining room lay, with the double set of glass doors that led to a patio and then to the beach. Someone had clambered up onto that patio. Someone was tapping on those doors.

And something, deep down in the core of her being, told her not to go see who it was.

So she stood, frozen and as silent as a grave, except for the effort it took to suck air into her lungs and let it out in shaky, uneven breaths.

Tap-tap-tap.

Come out, come out, wherever you are.

Jason wouldn't do that. He'd told her he would always knock at her front door, then ring the bell immediately after, so she could be sure it was him.

Tap-tap-tap.

Come out.

Panic wrapped around her like an invisible python, threatening to squeeze all the air out of her chest to make more room for the fear.

Tap-tap-tap.

Move, you stupid woman. Don't just stand there for him to find you.

Every instinct she possessed told her to be still, to keep whoever was outside from seeing her. But she knew she couldn't just freeze like a frightened rabbit. Because the fox was at her window, and he knew exactly where she was.

She forced herself to take a step forward, her muscles constricting in frightened protest. Then another, her breath growing jagged and so loud, it was the only thing she could hear. And still another, until she'd moved into the darkest shadows along the wall. Slowly she sidled toward the second doorway in the room, moving into the entryway, toward where a slim, corded phone sat on a table near the front door. Feeling her way across the near-pitch-black, windowless space, she stopped as her hip bumped painfully into a sharp corner. The table. Her hand scrabbled madly along its surface until her fingers finally made contact with the phone. She yanked the handset off its base.

But even before she got it up to her ear, she knew what she would hear. Or wouldn't hear.

No dial tone.

Choking back a frustrated cry, she jabbed repeatedly at the switch hook to no avail.

He'd cut her phone line.

Oh, God. She jerked her head up to look at the security system keypad. The little red LED light was still on, indicating it had switched to backup battery power. But without a working phone line, all it would do was sound an alarm inside her house—it wouldn't transmit the alarm signal to the company's central switchboard, since she hadn't yet had their new satellite backup system installed. No one would send the police. No one would hear her if she screamed for help.

She decided against turning on the interior alarm. This way it would go off if he broke in, providing an important warning.

Tap-tap-tap.

The noise grew more and more insistent, until it escalated into a pounding that thundered across her house.

Come out, come out, wherever you are.

Her eyes flicked to her heavy steel front door. She could make a run for it. She could try to get to her car, to a neighbor.

But what if they didn't open their doors? What if they left her outside alone…and he caught her? The image of the vicious-looking serrated knife embedded in the side of her house flashed through her mind.

Not like that. There was no way she was going to die like that.

Cell phone. He couldn't cut that line.

Bang! Bang! Bang!

Of course, that was in her purse. In the kitchen. And whoever was outside was growing more insistent.

She crept back into the living room, grateful for the pale light from the moon and the streetlamps streaming through her curtains. Edging toward the doorway to the kitchen, she braced herself.

Phone. What else was in there? What could she use?

Plastering her body against the wall next to

the doorway, she braced herself. The patio doors weren't covered by curtains or blinds. She'd see whoever was out there as soon as she walked into the room. And he'd see her.

So be it. She was no scared rabbit.

Whipping around the corner, she propelled herself into the kitchen, frantically scanning the counters for her purse. There, the grayish lump near the sink. She dived for it, scooping it off the counter and hugging it to her chest. As she backed away toward the living room, she stole a glance at the patio doors.

He wasn't there. Nothing obstructed her view of the cold Pacific. No one was beating on the glass.

Tightening her hold on her purse, she shoved her hand inside, rummaging through the contents until she felt the cool, slim shape of her cell phone at the bottom. She yanked it out, letting her bag drop to the floor with a thud. Using her thumbs, she punched in the number she knew by heart.

It rang once. Twice. Three times. And then, "Hi, this is Liz. Leave me a message."

"Liz," she hissed into the phone. "Liz, it's Addy. I think I'm in trouble. I'm calling 9-1-1—but please come over if you get this."

She punched the end button, looking over

her shoulder as she headed back into the living room. The patio remained deserted.

She hit 9-1-1 as she walked through the doorway, then turned around.

"9-1-1. What is your emergency?" a voice answered.

In the small gap between the living-room curtain panels, she saw a face. Looking at her.

She stumbled, and lost her grip on the phone. It fell out of her hands and skidded across the floor. She heard it slide under her couch and thump into the far wall underneath. The sound of several pieces scattering told her the battery had fallen out, giving the operator no time to trace the call.

She barely noticed, her focus entirely on the face in the window, wholly illuminated by the streetlights outside. It belonged to a man, and at first she thought he might have been a burn victim. But then she realized he was wearing a mask—a full overhead latex mask with the flesh disgustingly bubbled and scarred to give the effect that it had been fashioned from human skin. And while it was an obvious fake, that didn't make the effect much less terrifying.

She couldn't move. She could barely breathe as she and the monster outside stared at each other, waiting for someone to make the first move.

She had a ridiculous amount of money and an expensive security system on her house, but it still all boiled down to the fact that the only thing between her and those horrible eyes was a thin pane of glass. And with her phone deep under the sofa, she had no idea if she could summon help before he decided to come through it.

She was trapped.

Chapter Five

"Aren't you supposed to be home packing?" Liz rose from her desk to greet Daniel as he navigated through the other desks haphazardly arranged in the almost cavernous room that was home to the Homicide Department.

"Dive gear, T-shirts, swim trunks, flip-flops. Not like it's rocket science." Tomorrow he was supposed to be scuba diving in Cayman. Nothing but sand, sea, rum drinks with those blasted little umbrellas in them, and the endless coral precipices of the North Wall. After seventeen months of nothing but overtime and more overtime, it seemed like a dream—one that was starting to look more and more remote as the night wore on.

Especially since everything in him was shouting at him not to leave Adriana Torres alone.

"So you found our friend Stanley." He approached her desk and leaned his palms on it.

She tilted her chin down so the little gold reading glasses she wore slipped down her nose. All the better to shoot reproving looks at him over the rims. "I called to tell you that to ease your mind that we were making progress without you, not so you'd come in to pay your respects, you workaholic," she said.

"How long has he been waiting?"

Her thin mouth twitched upward in a satisfied smirk. "Only three hours. See, I so worried about who I'd take in with me to talk to him, since our best interrogator was going on vacation. And I needed to sit down and process that for a while."

"Right." The thought of Borkowski sitting down for a long worry fest was about as likely as the department group hugs Adriana had joked about that morning. "Where'd you pick him up?"

"One of his neighbors told us he likes to hang out at a Cabrillo Lanes up in Watsonville. We found him lurking at the bar, watching some teenage girls bowl. Perv." She yanked the glasses off her face and tossed them down on her rigidly organized desk.

She'd told him once that order helped her think. "So, now that you're here…?"

"I'd love to."

"I'm only going to say this once. You're supposed to be on vacation."

"Don't care."

With a satisfied gleam in her eye, Borkowski stood and headed toward the interrogation rooms in the back of the station. Daniel fell into step beside her. "So you realize you just volunteered to take the lead on this little talk?" she asked, her hand resting on the door handle to interrogation room number five. "If anyone can get something out of him this early, it's you."

He nodded. She turned the knob, and they went in.

Stan Peterson sat at a small metal table, his head bowed and his hands folded in front of him. He looked up as they entered, squinting under the garish glare of the fluorescent lighting and shifting his weight to grip the seat of the rusted folding chair with both hands. He hadn't changed out of his bicycle shorts and worn T-shirt since Daniel had seen him that morning, and from the smell of things in the cramped, windowless room, good old Stan had gotten in a workout sometime between now and then.

The officer who'd been on babysitting duty rose and left quietly, allowing Liz to take the seat across from Peterson. Daniel sat in the chair flanking him. Their chairs were the padded office-type, spalike compared to the rattletrap Peterson sat in. All the better to keep him off balance and vulnerable.

"So," Daniel began, purposefully sprawling out in his chair in an attempt to look casual. "I'm Detective Cardenas, and this is my partner, Detective Borkowski."

Borkowski raised an eyebrow at him, her face stony.

"Mind if I call you Stanley?" Daniel asked.

"Uh, Stan. I like Stan better." He shifted again in his seat, clearly uncomfortable.

"Sure." He whipped a pen out of his shirt pocket and pretended to make a note on the steno pad that had been sitting on the table. "So, do you know why you're here today, Stanley?"

With a slight scowl that he tried to hide, Peterson shook his head, his long stringy hair swinging slightly with the movement. He reminded Daniel of a less-flamboyant version of the hunchback in the *Rocky Horror Picture Show.* Minus the hunchback. "I haven't done anything wrong."

Daniel held up a hand. "Actually, we just wanted to see if you would help us out today." Borkowski handed him a manila folder, and he opened it, extracting a photo of Adriana. It must've been taken when James was still alive. She looked…the only word that did that smile justice was *radiant.*

Daniel reluctantly shoved the picture toward Peterson, willing him not to touch it. "You know this woman, right?"

Peterson's slightly bloodshot blue eyes widened at the sight of Adriana's face. He picked up the photo and pulled it close to his eyes. For a fleeting moment, Daniel got the distinct impression that the weirdo might want to lick the picture, and he wanted to rip it out of his hands and tear him apart for thinking whatever it was he was thinking about Adriana.

"Addy Torres?" Stan lowered the photo, though his fingertips lingered on Addy's face. "Sure. She teaches my morning yoga class at the Laughing Lotus downtown."

Borkowski leaned forward and glared across the table, her hair falling into her eyes. With a quick swing of her head, she sent it flying back. "She lets you call her Addy?"

"Sure." He nodded eagerly. "Sure. She told

me to call her that when we first met. I think I'm the only one, though. The other students call her Adriana."

Borkowski shot Daniel a meaningful look and sat back once more in her chair, her expression quickly shifting back to cool appraisal. But he didn't need Liz's unspoken message—it was crystal clear that Peterson was trying to establish himself as important to Adriana. Of course, all he actually was doing was establishing himself as a delusional whackjob.

"Has Ms. Torres by any chance confided anything to you about receiving any threats?"

Peterson ran his hands through his hair, his fingers briefly catching in the lank strands before he yanked them free. Not one of his more common self-grooming habits. His eyes darted left—possible sign of deception—and he opened his mouth twice and closed it again before finally forcing out a no.

Interesting. All signs pointed to the fact that Peterson was uncomfortable with the question. Might mean he was lying. But since Daniel hardly thought Adriana would confide in a smelly little weasel like Peterson, it was also likely that his discomfort was due to the fact that he didn't want to admit that she didn't talk to him about her personal business.

"Did you know she had a fiancé once?"

"No."

"He was a cop. Killed in the line of duty."

"Mmm. No, she's never mentioned him." That denial went easier for Peterson. "Guess she's over him now, right?"

Borkowski's eyes flickered, but otherwise her expression remained unchanged. If Peterson thought Adriana had gotten over James Brentwood that easily… Clearly, the guy had a rich and rewarding fantasy life.

"Sure, Stanley." He gave Peterson a reassuring smile. It made his face hurt. "Ms. Torres received a message this morning containing a picture of her deceased fiancé. Wouldn't know anything about that, would you?"

Peterson twitched his shoulders—a movement clearly meant to be a shrug, but it came off more as a sudden spasm. "Who'd do something like that?"

Narrowing his eyes, Daniel ran his hand along the five-o'clock shadow on his chin. Damn, he was tired. And he still hadn't had any coffee. "Don't know. What do you think?"

"He'd have to be a real nutcase to do that to hurt her." Sucking in his lips, Peterson tilted his head and thought for a moment. "But maybe it was just a friendly message.

Maybe someone wanted her to have a nice picture of him."

Borkowski's chin dropped, though she kept her mouth closed, her light brown bob falling once more into her eyes.

"He was dead in the picture," Daniel said.

"Ohhhhhhh."

"Yeah, ohhhh," he replied.

Daniel wheeled his chair closer to Stan, folding his arms on the table and leaning in as if to confide something in him. "See, Stanley, the only way someone could have gotten a picture of a Monterey cop shot in the line of duty was if he had killed the cop himself, or he hacked into our computer system."

There was a horrible screech of metal on tile as Peterson tried to shuffle his chair away from Daniel. But since he was already sitting in a corner of the room, he didn't have far to go.

Daniel just moved in closer. "And if he hacked our system…well, we have some badass experts on our side, you know? We've got our own tech geeks…" Daniel ticked off a finger. "The FBI would send its Computer Crimes agents down here in a flash if we told them our systems were being compromised. And did I mention Liz here is good friends with the guy who invented Interceptor?" He smiled genially, like a man having a pleasant conversation with no ulterior motives whatsoever. "You know, the FBI program that tracks billions of e-mails to sniff out terrorists?"

"I didn't—"

"Hang on. I'm on a roll here." Interrogation 101. Cut off all denials before they're fully voiced. Kept a suspect's confidence low and, more importantly, kept him from getting a chance to lawyer up. "So, as I was saying, if someone hacked into our systems to get a photo of Adriana Torres's deceased fiancé, we'll find him. *I'll* find him."

"But I wouldn't—"

"You like computers, Stan?"

Hunching over in his chair, Stan hitched up a shoulder in a smaller version of his jerky shrug. "No more than the next guy."

"That's not what your ex-girlfriend said," Borkowski interjected, rising up out of her contemptuous slouch. "You know, the one you threw a chair at."

Almost imperceptibly, Stan shrank away from her. "That was a misunderstanding—"

"She said you would be on the computer at least six hours a day after coming home from work." Liz narrowed her eyes at him. "And now that you're unemployed, I bet you're surfing porn all day…except when you take a yoga break."

"I like yoga."

"Don't most men?" Liz countered. Daniel narrowed his eyes at her. Now, if *he'd* said something like that, she would have been on him like a head-lice epidemic, for being sexist. Then again, she always had enjoyed playing up her role as Bad Cop.

Peterson swiveled to face Daniel. "Did you hear what she—"

Daniel cut him off midwhine. "Now, Detective, you know I like my asanas in the morning." The yoga reference seemed to relax Peterson slightly, as if he'd found an ally. Daniel almost smiled. "Look, Stanley, I'll be frank here. I was watching you this morning."

For a split second Stan Peterson's timid, half-witted expression changed so drastically, Daniel wasn't even sure what it was he'd seen. But then he realized that something that could only be described as pure rage had flashed across the man's face.

Maybe Stan Peterson wasn't as dopey as he'd have them believe.

"I saw you get out of that taxi a block after you'd gotten in it," Daniel continued. "You doubled back and watched Adriana Torres until she got in my car, and then you followed us in your blue Ford Taurus until I lost you."

"You…?" Stan let the question trail off.

"You asked her out today, and she turned you down, didn't she?"

Pressing his palms against his cheeks, Peterson dragged them quickly down his face in agitation. "No! I just—"

"But you must have known that was coming," Daniel pressed. "Isn't she a little out of your league, a beautiful woman like that? Smart. Successful."

Peterson hunched over, resting his forehead in his hands. Elbows perched on the tabletop, he cast his eyes down to stare at the space between them. Everything about his posture spelled defeat. Borkowski leaned in toward him, ducking her head to try to make eye contact with him. Daniel put a hand on Peterson's shoulder and leaned down so his face was level with Stan's.

"Why would someone leave a picture of her dead fiancé for Ms. Torres to find?" Daniel asked.

"I don't know," Peterson replied.

"The photo was hung near the doorway of her home with a hunting knife. The same method Elijah Carter, the serial killer who murdered Ms. Torres's fiancé, used to communicate with his targeted victims."

"Everyone knows how Brentwood died," Peterson muttered.

Daniel dropped his hand from Peterson's shoulder. There it was—blood in the water. He almost smiled.

"Thought you didn't know his name?" he asked quietly. "We never told you it was Brentwood."

Peterson's head shot up out of his hands. His mouth hung partway open, prominently displaying the gray snaggletooth in the front of his mouth. "Oh. Ummmm, yeah. Uhhhhh…"

"So I'm thinking you knew damn well how her fiancé died, and you or a friend of yours hacked into our police computer systems and found a photo of Brentwood," he continued. "Maybe you knew Adriana was going to reject you, and you wanted to pay her back."

Peterson tugged frantically at a greasy lock of hair at his temple.

"Or maybe you wanted to frighten her, so you sent her that note and then magically appeared in the parking lot outside her studio just as she arrived at work," Daniel presented another alternative that had Peterson shaking his head in an exaggerated way. "Her knight in shining armor."

At those words, Stan froze. An electrified silence descended on the room. Daniel could hear the man breathing deeply.

"I'm free to go anytime, aren't I?" Peterson finally said. His voice was deeper and more confident than it had been the entire time they'd been questioning him, as if another person had just taken over his body. His hand crept forward until his fingertips rested possessively on the photo of Adriana. "You don't have a warrant for my arrest, right?"

"No, we're just asking you a few questions."

"The next time you ask me questions, I'll want a lawyer present."

Daniel fought back a curse. In English and Spanish. "Sure," he said, careful to keep his voice neutral.

Adriana's face flashed in front of Daniel's eyes, suddenly, and without warning. Her pale face, her frightened eyes. The way she folded into herself. Not at all like the way she used to be—confident and carefree, like she'd been in the photo that Peterson had just started caressing again, instead of a beautiful loner shrouded in black.

He reached forward and yanked the photo out of Peterson's hands.

And then he thought of Brentwood. His coworker. His friend.

Peterson started to rise out of his chair. Daniel slammed his hand on the table, the noise making both Peterson and Liz jump. Kicking his chair back so it banged against the wall behind him, he stood, towering over Peterson. He barely registered Borkowski's low gasp of shock.

"You know, Stanley," he growled, "that photo of Brentwood appeared on Adriana's door, in a way Elijah Carter would have sent it. You'll read in the paper tomorrow about a murder victim who was killed in a manner very similar to how Carter dealt with his victims."

"Except the victim was also sexually assaulted," said Borkowski.

Daniel blinked but otherwise remained where he was, blocking Peterson's exit. He hadn't known the M.E. had confirmed that. Unless Borkowski was bluffing.

"If you had anything to do with Adriana's note or…anything else," Daniel said, playing along as if she hadn't just shocked the hell out of him, "you might want to make sure that lawyer you get is a good one. The medical examiner got some DNA evidence on our victim. And after bringing you in on a felony charge last year when you threw a chair at your girlfriend, we have your DNA for comparison."

Again, Stan's expression morphed into one that looked almost demonic—and not like it belonged to the stammering fool they'd been talking to minutes before. His eyes crinkled at the corners, and an evil smile spread across his now-placid face. "Well, now, Detective Cardenas, I believe that's impossible," he said calmly.

The note of amusement in his voice made Daniel's blood run cold.

"NICE JOB," Borkowski said as they strode down the hall toward their desks.

Daniel just grunted.

"Look, you're right. We didn't get enough out of him to arrest him yet—"

"Not unless we want to go up in front of a judge and say, 'He looked at us funny.'"

"As I was saying—" Liz shot him an exasperated look "—it wasn't a mistake, bringing him in this early. We might have set him on his guard a little, but at least now we know keeping an eye on Peterson wouldn't be a waste of time."

True.

"Was it true, what you said about the M.E. finding evidence of sexual assault?"

"No idea." She shrugged. "She made a guess at the scene—and I think she's right—but with the lab all backed up, we might find out for sure sometime next year."

"Fabulous," he said sarcastically.

"Tell me about it."

The state lab in Monterey County had been spectacularly backed up since Proposition 69 had been passed, mandating DNA collection from anyone arrested for a felony sex crime, murder, voluntary manslaughter. It also mandated DNA collection from anyone convicted of any felony, which was, if you looked at the bright side, why they had a sample from good old Stanley on file. Throwing a chair at someone in California was considered assault.

The sky was pitch-black outside the large bank of windows behind their desks. Liz said something about his not having time to pack before his early-morning flight to Cayman, but he couldn't have cared less about his vacation. He knew she wanted him to go—it had been a long time since he'd taken more than a few days to recharge from their constantly heavy caseload. But with someone copycatting Elijah Carter's methods of murder—maybe even Carter himself—now was not the time to leave the country. He went behind his desk and scooped up a handful of files, pounding their edges on the desktop until he held an even stack in his hands.

Liz perched her hip on a corner of his desk. "We've been working together a long time."

He grunted, piling more manila folders on top of the neat stack he'd made.

"You only tidy up this disaster of a desk when something's bothering you—which isn't often, Zen master," she said, pointedly emphasizing his nickname. She picked up a couple of stray hard candy wrappers and tossed them into a nearby wastebasket. "And, oh, wild guess here, I figure that something would be Stan Peterson?"

He paused to cock an eyebrow at her, then continued adding to his folder pile.

"Daniel, I've never seen you lose it in an interview like that. Not even a little. And from the guy who has definitely earned his department nickname, slamming a hand on a desk is practically a sign of total meltdown."

When he didn't respond, she ducked her head, employing the same techniques they'd used back in the interview room to catch his eye and hold it. "Taking this case a little personally, partner?"

"Carter killed a cop. Who was also my friend. I'll always take that personally." His hand accidentally knocked into the stack he'd been working on, and folders fanned across the desk, some spilling onto the floor. Disgusted, he threw down the file he'd been holding.

She pulled a pencil out of the mug-turned-holder on his desk and twirled it between her fingers, looking as if she wanted to say more. But then she closed her mouth and remained silent.

"Nothing fits," he said, thinking out loud. "Did Stan leave that note for Adriana? Is he tied to the Sanchez murder, or is he just a dead end. And what was up with Peterson's Linda Blair act back there?"

Stabbing the pencil back into the mug, Liz leaned toward him. "For a week, this case isn't your problem, Cardenas. You've been working yourself into the ground all year—don't think I haven't noticed." She held up a hand to stop what he was going to say next. "You need to go. This work gets to all of us after a while, and how are we going to catch this guy if our best interrogator burns out?"

A muffled beep shrilled from somewhere in the vicinity of Borkowski's desk, which sat next to Daniel's. She hefted herself off his desk and walked to her own. Pulling a set of keys out of her pocket, she quickly unlocked a drawer and tugged her purse out of it.

"Probably the kids," she said as she fished around for the off-duty cell phone that he knew was telling her she had a voice mail. "I was supposed to help them proofread their term papers..." Her voice trailed off as she punched in her voice-mail code, then pushed back her hair, holding the phone up to her ear.

He was just about to go back to stacking files and contemplating the travesty his interview with Peterson had been, when Borkowski's face abruptly lost color. She snapped her phone shut. "Addy's in trouble."

Daniel jumped to his feet, his desk chair slamming into the wall behind him. "How long ago did she leave that message?"

Borkowski frantically punched a few keys on the phone as they rushed to the building exit, apparently trying to check the call history. "Dammit, Daniel. Almost an hour ago."

ADRIANA GRIPPED the edge of her curtains and yanked them closed, blocking out the horrible face in her window.

But he was still there. And only a thin pane of glass sat between them.

Fear swirled in the pit of her stomach, slowly rising to spread out through her limbs and coil into a chokehold around her throat. She couldn't move; she could barely breathe.

Gun or knife? Bullet or torture? Which did he have planned for her?

Move.

She released her grip on the curtains and bolted for the front door. The tiny red light of her security system keypad winked at her in the darkness. The alarm would work. Maybe it would scare him away. Maybe one of her apathetic neighbors would be annoyed enough to call the police. She scrabbled around the keypad, searching for the three largest buttons, one of which would activate the shrill alarm.

Then she stopped.

Maybe the noise would be so loud, she wouldn't be able to hear him coming. Maybe by hitting that alarm, all she'd do is take away another one of her senses—with the power out, she was already practically blind.

Blind and deaf. Dumb and alone. With no

place to go but out. Where a man who may have killed James was waiting for her. Waiting to take her eyes.

Come out, come out, wherever you are.

Not like this. She wasn't going to go like this.

The entryway was nearly pitch-black, but she had the advantage since it was her house, and she'd placed every single object and piece of furniture in it. A few feet to the left of the doorway, a coatrack sat in the corner of the small room. Guiding herself along the wall, she swept her outstretched arm back and forth, until she felt the first brush of soft material from one of her jackets. Black wool, three-quarter length. Fit her like a glove. She knew this place well in the dark, and here in the dark she'd stay.

Sifting past the coats, she felt her hand connect with the walls behind it. And there, just below waist level, hidden behind the rack, sat a smooth, heavy Louisville Slugger—the perfectly balanced wooden bat her mother had given her when Adriana had made the high school fast-pitch team years ago.

Quiet as a graveyard, she tugged the bat from its hiding place, its weight reassuring in her hands. She'd had a .444 batting average back in high school—and she suspected her odds would be even better aiming at some maniac's giant melon.

Gripping the bat with both hands, she held it up against her shoulder. Her breath came out in heavy gasps, and she tried to control it, quiet it so she could hear what was going on around her.

The faintest sound of the ocean waves crashing against the rocks. A siren in the far distance. Her heartbeat in her ears.

She remained frozen for longer than she could have imagined, waiting, listening, trying to figure out which next move wouldn't get her killed. Maybe she could get her cell phone out from under the couch before he tried to come in. Maybe he'd run and she'd never have to use the bat. Maybe this was all just a warning.

Phone. She'd get her cell phone. Make sure help would come, make sure someone knew what was happening to her.

He cut your phone line. He cut your electricity. He's coming in.

Slowly she crept toward the living room, making her way across the hardwood floor with soft, carefully planted footsteps. Right foot. The waves outside crashed against the rocks. Left foot. The siren trailed off until she could no longer hear its high-pitched cry. Right foot. She could see the dim outline of the living-room window. No shadows danced behind the curtains, waiting for her to open them again and reveal what lay behind.

With a deep, shuddering inhalation, she dived toward the couch, her knees slamming painfully to the floor. Throwing the bat hard onto the couch cushions, she crouched low and slid her arm as far under the sofa as it would go, frantically feeling around for her phone. The tips of her fingers knocked into its slim form, but she'd hit it too hard, and it skidded away.

She tried again, lying across the floor so she could shove her hand even farther underneath the unyielding piece of furniture. Finally her hand connected with the phone, or a piece of it, and she used the tips of her fingers to bring it toward her.

And then she heard the sound of breaking glass raining down in the kitchen, as her security system's deafening alarm went off.

Chapter Six

Siren blaring, Daniel cranked the steering wheel of the Crown Vic sharply to the right, sending the car fishtailing into Adriana's driveway. He slammed the car into Park and jumped out, with his .40-caliber Smith & Wesson pointing at the sky. Jamming a clip inside, he chambered a round. Borkowski was by his side before he reached Adriana's front door, her own gun drawn and ready, as well.

The front door stood halfway open, and what they could see of the inside of the house was pitch-black. The house's shrill alarm had been tripped, and he wondered how apathetic her neighbors had to be to not pay attention to its deafening sound. Daniel pressed his back against the hinge side of the door frame, and Borkowski did the same on the other side. He caught her eye and nodded, and then kicked the door open, brandishing the Smith

& Wesson he held tightly in both hands. The door slammed back against the wall, and he swept the semiautomatic's barrel along the wall and up the stairwell that stood immediately in front of him. Liz did the same on her side of the room, then flicked on a heavy metal flashlight she'd had dangling from her belt. Still holding her gun out with her other hand, she ran the beam of light across the dark entryway and up the front stairs, to where the bedrooms were.

Clear.

Adriana had apparently trusted Liz with her alarm code, and Liz quickly turned it off. Since they were the only police on the scene, he assumed the phone line had been cut, and her security company had never gotten the message to call 9-1-1.

They worked quickly and in silence, checking every room on the first floor of the house. No sign of Adriana or Jason.

As they made their way back through the dining room on the way to the stairs in the front of the house, Daniel felt the slightest breeze hit the side of his face. He ran his hand along the edge of the sliding door, and discovered that it was cracked open less than a centimeter. He jerked his head toward the patio to let Liz know where he was headed. The door hissed on its track as he slid it open just enough so he could fit through. A cold wind blew off the water and across his face as he scanned Adriana's deserted backyard. Liz stepped out onto the patio behind him.

Far down the stretch of sand that led from Adriana's deck to the ocean, something large and unmoving lay between the rocks and the water. Large enough to be a body. Large enough to be Adriana.

He moved to the edge of the patio. A chill spread through him that had nothing to do with the icy wind.

Like the front yard, the sides of the deck were surrounded by shrubs that badly needed a trim. They, too, provided an ideal place for someone to hide and ambush them.

He glanced at Liz, and she nodded, knowing instinctively that she was to fall back and provide cover while he checked them.

Here we go….

He moved down the first step, trying to quell the impulse to look at the thing lying on the ground several feet away, to see if it looked anything like Adriana as he got closer. Damn, she'd been through so much. She didn't deserve this. She didn't deserve a ghost coming after her. She didn't deserve to die on that beach.

Second step. He leaned forward, looking as far around the overgrown shrubs as he could. No one was waiting directly at the bottom of the stairs.

Third and last step. He fanned his Smith & Wesson a hundred and eighty degrees in front of him, still keeping it close to his body in case someone tried to grab it. Nothing.

Liz moved to the left, checking out that side over the tops of the shrubs. He moved in the opposite direction.

"On your right!" she suddenly shouted.

He whirled around, his index finger tightening on the trigger of his gun. A shadowy figure stepped out from behind the shrubs. Instinctively, he sucked in his gut and bowed his body. He felt a whoosh of air across his chest, telling him he'd narrowly missed meeting the business end of a swinging blunt object.

With a high-pitched yell, his attacker swung again, and without thinking he tucked his shoulder in and rolled across the sand, coming to his feet quickly and well out of the weapon's reach.

"Daniel, don't shoot!" In a split second, he

reacted to Liz's voice as someone else shouted, "Come here, you mother—" It was Addy.

"Adriana, stop!" he yelled, gun pointed away from her. He held his forearm up in front of his face in case she decided to take another swing at him before she registered who he was.

She stopped the bat midswing, her body jerking forward with the halted momentum.

He'd often read the phrase "relief flooded through him," but he'd never felt it with so much intensity as he did at that moment, when he saw her, alive and whole. She let the top of her bat drop to the sand.

"Daniel?" The pitch and volume of her voice were back to almost-normal levels, and her chest heaved up and down as she stared at him in disbelief. She reached up and pushed a stray lock of dark hair out of her eyes.

"For heaven's sake, Addy, he could have shot you!" Borkowski hustled down the stairs to where Adriana stood, staring blankly at the two of them and clearly in shock. "What were you doing hiding in the bushes like that?"

In two strides Daniel was by Adriana's side. Her breathing grew louder and faster and her entire body started to tremble. She had a death grip on her bat, and refused to let go even when he tried to take it out of her hands. She let out a strange hiss, and it took him a moment to figure out that she was trying to say something.

"What is it, Addy?" Liz asked, wrapping her arm around Adriana's shoulders. Daniel leaned in closer, fighting the urge to take her into his arms until she stopped shaking.

"Jason." She lifted the bat until it pointed toward the mass they'd seen earlier on the beach. The tide had crept closer, and water lapped at the edges of whatever or whoever lay a few yards from where they stood.

Oh, no.

"Keep her safe," he barked at Liz, then turned back to the body on the beach. His vision tunneled until the only thing he could see was the body in front of him. He hadn't even given Jason a second thought since he'd heard Adriana's message.

When he finally reached the body, the wet sand catching and holding his shoes like glue, he grabbed the first part he could reach and pulled it toward him.

Jason flopped over on his back, his eyes wide-open and staring at the sky.

"Oh, no. Come on, buddy. Don't do this."

Falling to his knees, Daniel shoved his gun in his holster and pressed two fingers against the side of Jason's thick neck. He moved them frantically across the big man's skin, trying to find a damn pulse. "Jace, come on."

Behind him, he barely registered Borkowski calling in the scene. Pressing his hand on Jason's forehead, he pushed down, so the man's chin tilted upward and his airway opened. He was just about to start CPR when he felt something grip his wrist.

"I always knew—"

Daniel jerked upward. His friend looked waxy and half-dead in the moonlight, but his eyes were now trained directly on Daniel's face.

"—you had…the hots…for me," he managed weakly, then his head lurched forward as he erupted in a series of watery-sounding coughs. A small trickle of blood pooled at the corner of his mouth. "Don't…kiss me, man."

"Borkowski! We need an ambulance, stat!" he shouted over his shoulder, then turned back to Jason. "Where are you hurt?"

With a fierce grimace, Jason lifted his meaty hand off of his rounded stomach, revealing a hole in his sweatshirt, which was soaked completely through with blood. Dammit, that looked bad.

"Got shot… Fell off deck… Cracked head." Jason stopped talking to catch his breath, which grew shallower and more labored with each word he forced out. "Don't know…how I got here."

"Don't talk, Jace." Daniel removed his jacket, wadding it up and pressing it against the bullet wound in Jason's stomach. He kept his face neutral and his voice calm, not wanting to tip off his friend to the severity of his wound. Jabbering on about nothing, in an attempt to keep Jason from losing consciousness, he started mentally examining the newest pieces of the puzzle.

Someone had shot Jason. And while he'd been unconscious, they'd tried to drag him toward the ocean, most likely to drown him.

And only someone extremely strong or equipped with a forklift could have carried or dragged a man as solid as Jason at least twenty-five feet down the beach, in sand, no less. The guy weighed at least three hundred and fifty pounds, most of it solid muscle.

"Find…the kid."

"Kid? Wait, don't answer that." Jason sounded way too weak. Asking the questions

Daniel was dying to ask would only make things worse, could even kill him. If the person who'd broken into Adriana's house had tried to drown Jason when he was down, it might mean Jason had seen something.

Jason shook his head, opening and closing his mouth and obviously trying to finish his train of thought.

"Look at me." Daniel got right in his friend's face. "Stop. Talking. I'm not kidding around here."

"Kid—" another coughing jag gripped Jason, which finally made him decide to take Daniel's advice and shut the hell up so he didn't suffocate on his own blood.

"Just breathe, man. Keep it shallow. That's it."

As the shrill sound of several sirens coming closer pierced the air, Adriana crouched down on the sand. She took Jason's hand, looking into his face as he struggled noisily to breathe.

She looked up at Daniel, but he shook his head before she could ask him how Jason was doing. He didn't want his friend to hear the answer. She understood his unspoken message, because she remained silent.

Finally he heard the sounds of doors

slamming and people shouting. He heard Liz giving orders. Then two EMTs with a stretcher approached them and took over. As Liz pulled Adriana back toward the house, Daniel quickly described Jason's injuries to the emergency team. They struggled to get the stocky bodyguard onto the stretcher. It took four EMTs and himself to heft him across the sand and into the waiting ambulance.

His pants heavy with water and the random clumps of wet sand still stuck to them, Daniel headed back inside the house himself. A few officers hustled around, securing the area around the house and setting up huge, portable lamps to illuminate the scene. Ahead of him Lockwood and his partner headed next door to start canvassing the neighbors.

He should have been right there with them. He should have been knocking on doors or looking for clues to the identity of the bastard that had almost killed his friend. But all he wanted was to see Adriana.

Bounding up the patio steps, he pushed his way past the sliding-glass doors and into the house, following Borkowski's deep voice into the living room. As he walked into the room, Adriana looked up, her face tight with emotion.

"Oh, God, Daniel."

Whether it was the too-vulnerable look on her face or the fact that she'd called him Daniel instead of Detective, he crossed the room in two steps and gripped her shoulders, pulling her to her feet. Instinct took over, and he wrapped his arms around her. Her body molded perfectly against his, her arms wrapping around his neck, one slim hand curling around the back of his skull. He bowed his head into her hair. It still smelled like flowers.

"I mean, Detective," she whispered against the skin above his collar, clinging to him for all she was worth. Her body felt rigid with lingering fear, and he held her tightly, as if he could protect her from the thing that had taken down a man three times her size, trained in hand-to-hand combat by the best the US military had to offer.

"What's up with the Zen master? That his girlfriend or something?"

He glanced up to see a couple of cops walk through the room, staring at him.

"Never seen him so much as pat a vic on the head before, you know? And isn't he supposed to be on vacation?"

Suddenly self-conscious, he straightened to his full height, and Adriana took that as a cue to back out of his embrace. The officer who'd spoken grinned at him and headed into the kitchen.

"Sorry," Adriana murmured.

"Ignore them," he replied. Out of the corner of his eye, he noticed Liz squinting at them, looking half-puzzled, half-amused. He followed his own advice and ignored her, too, leading Adriana to the couch and helping her sit down. He sat next to her.

"Can you tell me what happened?"

She described how her power and her phone line had been cut, disabling her alarm system's connection to the security company's dispatchers and leaving her isolated and vulnerable. She told him about the face she'd seen in the window, the sound of breaking glass coming from the back of the house.

As she spoke, she curled her long legs into a lotus position, clenching her hands in her lap, folding into herself as if she wanted to disappear…again.

"So you heard breaking glass. Then what happened?"

"I called 9-1-1 on my cell phone, but I dropped it before I could tell them anything, and it broke apart. I still don't know where the battery is." She rubbed her arms. "I grabbed my bat."

Monterey County dispatchers could trace cell phones, but it took time. "Where did you go?"

"The sound came from the back of the house, so I went out the front door." She looked down at her lap, and he noticed that she was clenching something tightly in her hands. "I was planning to start banging on doors, but I saw someone running toward me from the street. Somehow I knew I had to get away from him. So I ran behind the house. I heard a gunshot, saw Jason go down." She pressed her lips together, clearly angry, but whether at Jason's would-be killer or herself, he couldn't say.

"I ran to him, tried to stop the bleeding, but it wouldn't stop, and it was getting harder for him to breathe the longer I sat there with him. So I went back to see if I could get help, but I could hear someone inside." She paused to rub her fingers around her temple, more out of a nervous habit than anything else, he guessed. She stared at her hands. "I hid in the bushes, trying to listen, to figure out where he was headed, whether I could get past without him catching me if I went to the neighbor's.

I heard the sirens, but I didn't hear where he went. Then you and Liz came outside, and…"

"And you came around the bushes, screaming like a banshee," he finished.

She didn't smile, instead regarded him with a distant curiosity. "How did you know? When I swung that bat at you…" Her eyebrows knitted together as she studied his face. "With your training, you should have shot me."

The left side of his mouth quirked upward. "You scream like a girl."

A faint ghost of a smile crossed her face, but then her light brown eyes clouded again. She looked…haunted. And a protective rage like nothing he'd ever known flared inside him.

"What's in your hand, Addy?" he asked gently.

Slowly she brought her right hand up to chest level and unfurled it, blinking rapidly as she studied the thing she'd been holding.

A pair of wire-rimmed glasses, with a spiderweb network of cracks on one lens.

James Brentwood's glasses.

"Oh, hell," he breathed. The photo—that's what had felt so off about it. They'd never found James's glasses when they'd run the crime scene after he'd been shot and killed in Iris Canyon Park. The person who'd taken the picture would have been the person who'd taken the glasses, before the police had found Brentwood's body.

These glasses had been in that photo that had been impaled near Adriana's door earlier that morning. That photo had been taken by James Brentwood's killer, four years ago.

Dammit to hell, those glasses meant only one thing. Elijah Carter was back. And he was coming for Adriana.

Daniel opened his mouth, to tell her he'd keep her safe, tell her he wouldn't leave her side. He'd die before he'd let Elijah Carter and his knives and his fishing line and his twisted, murderous compulsions get past him to her. He'd give up his job to keep her safe. Someone had to be near her 24/7, because the man who was after her was the most dangerous, most psychopathic individual who had ever walked the planet. And Daniel didn't want to examine too closely why that someone had to be him.

He wanted to tell her he'd stay with her, to promise her he'd be with her to the end, but then her fingers curled around James Brentwood's glasses, and she brought them to her, resting them against her heart. A message, a reminder.

She wasn't his to protect.

She wasn't his.

"WE NEED TO GET YOU some protection. Now." Liz kept her voice at a normal, conversational volume, but there was no mistaking the steel in that order.

Adriana tried to occupy her mind with the inconsequential, concentrating on the cool wire and broken-glass texture of James's glasses in her hand, the sound of the door clicking shut as someone closed it, the rough feel of the wood floor planks beneath her bare, sandy feet. Surface. Keep everything on the surface. Don't think about it. Don't think.

In the background, amidst all the activity and the voices of the cops in and around her house, she could hear the sound of the ocean. High tide, crashing against the rocks.

As inevitable as the reality that she'd been denying up until this moment: Elijah Carter was back. And he was looking for her. To finish what he'd started. To kill other women, in the most horrible ways.

She sensed movement and turned to see Liz with her head bowed, squeezing the bridge of her nose, her chin-length hair partially obscuring her face. As if sensing Adriana's gaze, she jerked her head up, her face pale and drawn.

"How can this community go through this again?" Liz murmured.

How can we *go through that again?*

The unspoken question hung in the air as the silence stretched on, until Liz smacked her hands on her thighs and pushed herself up to standing.

"Are you scared?" Addy didn't know what prompted her to ask that question. In all the years that she'd known Liz Borkowski, she'd learned that the woman would probably rather quit the force and take up knitting than admit weakness.

But Addy had underestimated the other part of her character that made Liz who she was—her blunt honesty.

"I'm terrified."

At Liz's pronouncement, Daniel eased off the couch and walked across the room, pretending to be engrossed in admiring the few photos she had hung on the wall. He and Liz probably didn't emote together very often.

When Addy looked back at Liz, she saw that her friend had unconsciously assumed the universal cop fighting stance, bracing one leg behind the other, her body turned slightly sideways. It made them a smaller target,

James had long ago explained. Her right hand hovered over the holster where her gun rested. She may well admit to fear, but she'd never show it if she could help it.

"Therefore, we need to get you some protection," Liz added.

Ah, now it made sense. Her friend's moment of weakness had a noble motive behind it. Of course.

And Addy knew exactly what "some protection" meant—Liz had been on her forever to buy a gun. *A single woman living alone should be able to take care of herself.* But she hated guns, couldn't stand the thought of having something whose sole purpose was violence in her house.

Then again, if The Surgeon really was alive, she doubted that some small, ladylike pistol alone could stop him.

Pressing her palms against her cheeks, Adriana tugged them slowly downward as she stared blindly at the sofa table on the opposite wall, at the photo resting on it of her and a man with rumpled hair and a smile that had never failed to make her heart skip a beat. *Remember. Remember what he's done.*

"You know," she said, "I promised myself

after James died that I wouldn't let anyone change the way I lived, that I wouldn't be afraid all the time."

"You have to change, Adriana. Elijah Carter is no ordinary criminal." Daniel had slowly made his way back to them and had been quietly hanging out on the fringes of their conversation for the past few minutes. All the same, suddenly hearing his deep voice was startling, because he'd been quiet for so long. "We can put you in a safe house—"

"No." She shook her head, jabbing her index finger toward him in an I-mean-business kind of way. "No. That I won't do. I won't give up my job, my house, everything just to live this cowardly, shrunken life." It was already cowardly and shrunken enough.

"There's nothing cowardly about not wanting to be a serial killer's next victim." On the outside, Daniel looked as Zen masterlike as always, his body preternaturally still, the expression on his handsome face as placid as if they'd been discussing the weather. But then something flashed in his green-and-gold eyes—something worried and almost pleading. And that frightened her more than anything that had happened tonight.

"I'm going to go walk around," Liz said

abruptly. She turned to Daniel. "So, about that vacation—"

"What vacation?" he replied softly.

"I was afraid you'd say that. Here's me, trying to talk you out of it." She paused. "Okay, see you later." With that, she walked briskly out of the room, the cracks in her tough-cop facade no longer visible.

Once Liz had left the room, Addy turned to Daniel. "What do you mean, 'what vacation'?"

Daniel hooked a finger under his collar and tugged it away from his neck—only the second nervous tic she'd ever seen him display. Ever. "Ah, I was going to take a week off and hang around the house, get some work done in the garage, finally watch all six episodes of the *Star Wars* saga in order on my big-screen, that kind of thing."

Why did she have the feeling he was lying? "And now?" she prompted.

"Now I am going to strongly recommend—" he emphasized the last two words "—that you spend it with me."

Por el amor de Dios. She didn't know what was the matter with her, but her entire body flushed hot when he said that, as if he'd been asking her on a date—in an admittedly cavemanlike fashion—rather than speaking as Officer Safety.

Then he smiled at her, a slightly off-center full-on grin, perfectly straight teeth flashing white against his golden-brown skin. "I promise I don't snore."

But can you promise I won't fall for you?

"How long?" she managed, her voice cracking slightly, to her utter mortification. Maybe she'd just have to deal with him for a day or two, and then they'd assign someone married and near retirement to babysit her.

"As long as it takes."

A day? A week? Months? Years? How long would she be like this again, living in fear and reliving the past? "You know, every time we saw a cop show on TV where the police offered protection to a civilian, James would start going on about how no police force had the budget or the man- or womanpower to offer personal security services." She narrowed her eyes at him as she studied his face. "You're giving up your vacation for me. Unpaid."

He didn't respond.

"And when you're back on the books in a week, and The Surgeon is still at large? Are you going to start collecting unemployment because I'm afraid to be alone?"

"Again, *Carter's* no ordinary criminal," he finally said, emphasizing the killer's given name. "If he's stalking you now, it's because he's coming for you later. That's his pattern. And I wouldn't be doing my job if I left you and just promised to send a few patrol cars down your street every four hours." He paused, then said, "Let me do this, Adriana. Let me do my job."

Job. It was just a job. She was a job. That's all.

"I really want to tell you to go enjoy *Star Wars* and forget about me, but—" she looked down at her hands, started picking at her cuticles "—knowing Liz and you are afraid… If you think protection is what I need to stay—" Oh, God, she couldn't finish that sentence.

"I do. So does Liz."

When she didn't respond, he knelt down before her, catching her arms with his strong, brown hands and forcing her to look at him. If superheroes really did exist, they'd look like Daniel, all truth and justice and really great cheekbones. They'd make you feel that nothing bad could touch you as long as they were around. He must have known the effect he had on people. He must have known she couldn't resist the sanctuary—real or illusory—that he offered. From Carter. From her nightmares.

"You asked me how long," he said. "Once you say yes, I'm with you until the end, Adriana. However long it takes until we catch him."

But there could be another end to this story. It could end like the last one, with him being the one on the ground and a bullet in his back. She couldn't say a word, which he seemed to mistake for doubt in his ability to protect her.

"I'll keep you safe. I swear."

"What about Jason?" she asked, fighting off an urge to grab him by his broad shoulders and shake some sense into him. "He's a lot bigger than you, and Carter flattened him."

"He won't flatten me." His mouth quirked upward in the crooked half smile she was starting to recognize. "There's one other difference between Jason and me."

"Which is?"

"Nothing's going to make me leave your side."

Oh, my.

"Yes." She barely realized she'd agreed until the word shot out of her mouth, against her better judgment. Coward. Stupid, frightened coward. He didn't deserve to be involved in this. He didn't deserve to die because of her. And if there was one thing she knew well, it was how fragile life was, and how easily Elijah Carter could snuff it out.

As if he could read her thoughts, something softened in his deep hazel eyes. He reached up to trace her jawline with his hand, making the barest contact with her skin. It stole her breath all the same.

"Ma'am?" Another detective, probably in his fifties with sandy-brown hair shot with gray stepped forward. He'd obviously been listening to the whole exchange, which made her feel like squirming away from Daniel. But Daniel didn't drop his hold on her, instead looking calmly over his shoulder at the cop.

"Lockwood," he said in greeting.

"Hey, Cardenas." He turned back to Addy. "I just wanted to assure you, you can trust him with your life. He'd die before he let anyone get to you."

That was exactly what she was afraid of.

Chapter Seven

"Do you have to have the volume up when you're looking at that?" Adriana padded into the living room, her hair damp from a shower and her body wrapped up in a plush white robe. Daniel had to look away, before he started imagining what it would be like to untie that robe and skim his hands all over what was inside it.

"Sorry. I didn't think you'd be up this early." Running his fingers through his hair in case he looked like Don King, he tapped a few keys on his laptop with his free hand. The electronic screams coming from the Web site he'd been surfing abruptly cut off.

"Thanks." She turned and disappeared through the kitchen doorway.

Truth was, he was glad she was up. The sooner they got her packed and somewhere else, the better. He'd meant to take her to his condo last night, but by the time they'd finished processing the scene and he'd arranged for a twenty-four-hour repair service to fix her broken window, she'd fallen asleep. He hadn't had the heart to wake her after all she'd been through, so he'd just carried her to bed and had camped out on the couch.

She looked beautiful when she was asleep. Peaceful.

She returned several minutes later, holding a steaming mug out to him.

"If that's coffee, I'm going to ask you to marry me," he informed her matter-of-factly as he took the mug from her. "Just ignore me—I'll be back to normal once the caffeine hits." He looked inside, and probably would have done a dance of joy if it hadn't been for the raging withdrawal headache he'd had for the past twenty-four hours. He took a drink—hot and strong as hell, just how he liked it. "Marry me?"

A reluctant smile played at the corners of her full mouth, giving him the impression that she was debating whether to laugh or tell him to go to hell.

She opted for careful politeness instead. "What are you doing on that awful Web site?"

He folded the laptop screen down, so it

snapped shut, hiding the disturbing images from her.

Popping open the diet cola she'd brought in with her, she tucked herself into the end of the couch nearest his chair. She'd twisted her hair up, using two chopsticks to hold it in place. All the better to show off her swanlike neck.

Focus. He needed to focus.

"Trying to find out who would post pictures of you looking like a murder victim," he said, getting his head back where it belonged. "I hacked into the source code, but it's going to take me a while to get through it. So far it looks pretty straightforward, but…."

"Straightforward?" She snorted. "Maybe if you're one of the Manson family."

At least she still had her sense of humor. "I meant the code itself, not what they did with it," he said. "I've also been working on tracing its origins."

"Detective Cardenas—"

"Adriana—" He interrupted, gesturing at the navy cotton shorts and white T-shirt he was wearing. "In case you haven't figured it out, I'm in my boxers, in your living room, and I'm officially off the clock. Call me Daniel."

She clutched the lapels of her bathrobe tightly together and looked away, but not before he'd noticed that he'd made her blush. Not wanting to make her uncomfortable, or think any more about her neck and his mouth on it, he got back down to business. Maybe once they were fully clothed, this would get easier. "Whoever created that site set it up remotely on a South Korean server, through a dummy account in the Netherlands. It dead ends there, but we should be able to trace it… eventually."

"Did you sleep?"

Her question surprised him. She had a violent killer who'd set his sights on her, and she was wondering if he'd gotten his beauty sleep. "I don't sleep much. Ever."

She blushed again, and he wanted to kick himself. He hadn't meant it like *that.* "Liz says I'm a workaholic. Which is saying a lot, since she's racked up her share of overtime, too."

"Oh." She took a sip of her cola, looking at him over the edge of the can. "But I would guess that you normally sleep more than an hour."

"And here I thought I was being quiet."

She waved him off. "I woke up at exactly 2:37 a.m. and couldn't sleep after that, either." Reaching forward, she flipped his laptop screen back open.

"Adriana, maybe you shouldn't—"

"It's okay. Maybe I'll see something you didn't, since they are pictures of me." She scrolled down the screen, to some of the more dead-looking ones. "Or my head, at least."

He had to hand it to her, she had guts, looking at that Web site again. Most people wouldn't have been able to stomach the images more than once, if that—especially knowing they were likely meant as a direct threat.

"'Trembling hands reach out to stop me, she vomits lies she's learned by rote,'" she read. "What lies?"

"Whoever posted this sees himself as intimately connected to you," he said. "Even if it's the intimacy between the person inflicting the violence and the victim." He leaned in closer to see what she was seeing. God, he wanted to catch this guy. "Have you ever had someone in your life who got angry at you, accused you of lying to them?"

She shook her head, still staring at the screen. "No. Except James. He called me a liar whenever I told him he looked handsome." She started blinking rapidly. He gave her a minute to regroup.

"Maybe you shouldn't—" He started to close the screen once more.

"No." She put her hand over his, trying to stop him. He just waited, watching her.

She swallowed, took her hand away. "It's okay. I can handle it with the sound turned down. There's something I wanted to tell you."

She concentrated too intently on scrolling down to the only other picture that had a caption—the one where the victim was tied to a bed and a knife sliced across her neck every few seconds.

"'And I whisper that I love her with my knife held to her throat,'" she murmured, then turned to him. "This is going to sound really strange, but the two captions seem to go together—the rhythm's mostly iambic."

"Am I supposed to know what that means?" he asked.

"Not unless you like poetry." She backed away from the computer and smiled. And he realized how much he liked seeing her smile. She shifted in her seat, so engrossed in her topic, she seemed to have forgotten the reason they were discussing it. "Iambic is how poets describe that particular rhythm—unstressed syllable, followed by a stressed syllable. Like a heartbeat. Ba-BUM, ba-BUM, ba-BUM."

"So what you're saying is that the threat is written like a poem?"

She nodded. "Exactly. '*Trem*bling *hands* reach *out* to *stop* me.' Okay, the rhythm is off in a few places, like 'trembling'—I'm not saying it's a very good poem. But see what I mean?"

He quoted softly:

"Come live with me, and be my love,
And we will some new pleasures prove
Of golden sands, and crystal brooks:
With silken lines and silver hooks."

A faint blush crept up her cheeks, and he noticed that she was having a hard time looking at him.

"That it?" he asked. There was something really wrong about flirting with her when they'd just been looking at what amounted to veiled threats against her. But he wanted to see her smile again. He wanted to take her mind off all of this, even for just a few seconds.

"Yes, that's it." She nodded, licked her lips. "John Donne?"

"Yeah. One called 'The Baite.'"

"You don't know what iambic is, but you can quote Donne?" Her mouth twisted up in an amused smirk. Close enough.

"I was a criminal-justice major—I only paid attention in English when it interested me."

"Get a lot of dates out of that one?"

He laughed. "A few."

"You should do that more often," she said, watching him intently.

A moment like that couldn't last, not with his computer flashing between them like a damned homicidal elephant in the room. She dropped her gaze, glancing at the computer. "So, anyway—" her jaw clenched, and she hugged her arms close to her chest, the light tone gone from her voice "—those lines are in iambic heptameter—seven beats mostly in a ba-BUM, ba-BUM rhythm. As I said, it goes off in a few places. I read it and, much as I don't want to go there, I think there's more to it."

He tilted the computer screen toward him, clicking down the screen. "'*Trem*bling *hands* reach *out* to *stop* me, she *vom*its *lies* she's *learned* by *rote*,'" he read, stressing every second syllable just as she'd said. "'And I *whis*per that I *love* her with my *knife* held to her *throat*.' Wow, you're right."

"Yeah, it sticks in your head, in a really annoying way."

He had to admit, she might be on to something. "We searched this place pretty thoroughly last night. I don't think there's anything else here, but…maybe there's more to come."

"It makes sense that there would be," she agreed.

He had to hand it to her—it wasn't something he and Liz would have noticed right away. "You should have been a cop."

"Actually, Liz always tells me I should just go on a game show," she said. "My head is full of useless trivia."

Before he could reassure her that what she'd contributed was hardly useless, she smacked her hands on her thighs and stood up. "I'm going to get dressed and pack. There's a spare bath upstairs, if you'd like to shower. I've already laid out some towels for you, and soap, shampoo. Anything else you need?"

He shook his head and watched her graceful walk as she headed toward her bedroom suite. The woman knew how to walk, that was for damn sure.

Once she was out of sight, he pulled the rest of his clothes back on, then went upstairs to splash some water on his face and brush his teeth with the new brush she'd left him. He figured he'd shower when they were safely back at his apartment—he'd be no good to

Adriana if someone tried to break in and he couldn't hear them over running water.

Several minutes after he got back downstairs, she returned to the living room, wheeling a suitcase behind her. She set it just inside the living-room doorway. "Can I make you some breakfast? If you just tell me what you like...."

He barely registered what she was asking. She was dressed in her standard funeral-march attire—a pair of flare-leg black pants and a black tank with a gray wraparound sweater. Holding back her damp, dark chestnut hair, however, was a folded, brilliant red scarf, tied behind one ear, so the ends trailed over one shoulder.

Driven forward like a man possessed, he moved toward her. And when he stopped directly in front of her, stepped into her space, she didn't back away.

Reaching up, he fingered the ends of her scarf, drinking in her face, her brown eyes. Her mouth, full and deep pink without makeup, dropped open slightly, and he wondered what she would do if he tilted his head, like that. If he came even closer...

He watched the movement of her throat as she swallowed. "Daniel," she whispered, bracing one hand on his chest. He could feel her breath on his face. Her hair smelled like spices.

He looked down at her hand. Too much, too soon? He wasn't sure, but he couldn't take that chance. The silk of her scarf slipped through his fingers like water as he took his hand away. "Beautiful," he said softly.

She reached up to play with the ends of her scarf, using it as an excuse not to look him in the eye. "It's old," she said. "I've had it forever."

I didn't mean the scarf. But the words felt clichéd even though he meant them more than anything. So he left them unspoken.

"We should go." Back to business. Back to what she would see as safe ground. "We can have breakfast at my place."

"You cook?" She relaxed a little as he backed off to a more socially acceptable distance.

"Sure. Ramen noodles or mac and cheese? Oh, I have some Frosted Flakes, too."

"Uhhhh…"

"Kidding. I make a mean batch of French toast." He walked around her and grabbed the handle of her suitcase.

She followed him to the front door, picking up her purse and keys from the antique telephone table in the entryway. That reminded him—they'd need to call the phone company later to repair her line.

He pulled the front door open, just as he heard a car door slam. "Addy, get back in the house." He used his body to block her exit, shielding her as Stan Peterson got out of his Ford Taurus and crossed the street, coming toward them. His stringy hair flew out behind him as he strode into Adriana's front yard with angry purpose.

Instead of going back inside, Adriana put her hand on Daniel's shoulder and peered around him, gasping when she saw Stan.

"Addy, what's he doing here?" the little creep asked, jerking a thumb at Daniel and craning his neck to better see around him.

"Stan, he's a friend of mine—"

"Don't reason with him. He won't get it," Daniel murmured to her, still keeping himself between her and Peterson. If the guy heard him, he didn't give any indication of it.

"What are you doing here, Stanley?"

Stan screwed up his face, curling his upper lip so his snaggletooth was in full view. "I'm not talking to *him*, Adriana."

"He'll talk to me if I wipe your driveway with him," Daniel muttered as he stepped forward.

"It's okay. I'll ask him," she whispered in his ear. Then, she raised her voice to address Stan. "Why did you come here, Stan?"

"We had a date. One o'clock, remember?" he whined. Daniel had to admit, the guy looked pretty pathetic, standing there with his arms flailing at his sides, a sad-sack look on his face. "We were going for ice cream," he continued.

Never mind that it was October and getting a little cold for ice cream.

Adriana's dark eyebrows drew together, her forehead wrinkling in sympathy.

"Don't feel sorry for him," Daniel began.

"Oh, Stan, I'm sorry." She moved around him and took a step toward Peterson. Daniel moved right with her. "I didn't mean to confuse you. I thought I said I couldn't make it."

Peterson shook his head emphatically, looking like a spoiled kid who didn't want to eat his vegetables. A very big, very scuzzy-looking kid. "We had a date, Addy. I was very specific about when I'd be here."

"Stan, I don't think—"

"You didn't think," he said, still shaking his head. The movement grew jerky and more and more agitated. "Or you wouldn't have stood me up."

Classic stalker behavior, the whole refusing to take no for an answer. Peterson might look too pathetic to have terrorized Adriana last night. He might look too scrawny to have dragged Jason from her house to the water. But that didn't mean he wasn't dangerous. "She said no, Stanley. She's not interested in you."

Peterson grew still, and the glare he gave Daniel was pure malevolence. "We had a date."

"You had jack, Stanley. You wanna know how I know?" Reaching for Adriana's hand, he took her slim fingers in his. When she looked at him in surprise, he willed her to trust him. And she didn't protest when he held on to her. "She's seeing me."

Stan's mouth worked as several seconds ticked by. "Is this true, Addy?" he finally managed.

She nodded, tightening her grip on Daniel's hand. "Yes. Yes, it's true. We've been dating for a while now."

He stared at them in disbelief, then finally turned away. But not before Daniel heard him mumble "slut" under his breath.

Daniel shot forward, grabbing one of Peterson's arms and twisting it behind his back. Gripping the back of the man's collar,

Daniel steered him unceremoniously back to his car, shoving him down across the hood face-first.

"Don't ever let me hear you call her that again, you got me, Stanley?" he snarled in the man's ear. "Because when I'm off duty, what I do is my business."

Peterson struggled against his hold. "Are you threatening me, Detective Cardenas?" he grunted, emphasizing Daniel's title.

Damn straight. But it would be very stupid to admit it. With one final push into the hood, he let Peterson go. Throwing his palms in the air, he backed off, knowing he looked like one of those overly aggressive TV cops and still unable to stop snarling at the man. "Wouldn't dream of it, Stanley. Just letting you know who's watching out for her."

Peterson picked himself up off his car hood, scrubbing his sleeve across his mouth. He didn't look angry anymore, just strangely defeated.

"Are we clear?" Daniel pressed.

Peterson responded with another question. "Do you love her?"

Freaking psycho. Moods changed on a dime.

All the same, he found himself responding. "With everything I've got."

Head bowed, Peterson slunk toward his car, opening the driver's-side door. Just when Daniel was starting to feel sorry for the freak, he turned back to Adriana, who had been watching the whole scene from her front yard. "Addy, he can't protect you. Only I can do that," Peterson shouted at her.

"We need to go, Adriana." Daniel was by her side in two strides, hustling her toward the car. The farther Adriana stayed from this head case, the better.

"I came here to save you, Addy!" Stan called as they got into Daniel's car. "I'm the only one who can."

Chapter Eight

Daniel gunned the engine, and they sped away, leaving Stan standing in the middle of the road, watching them go.

The car veered sharply to the left, and Addy yelped as she gripped the back of her seat to keep from slamming into the door. Behind them, one of her teenage neighbors started doing figure eights in the middle of the street on his skateboard.

She turned back around to face front. "How close did you get to hitting that kid?"

Daniel picked up his aviators off the dash and put them on. "Not that close. Came out from behind a car all of a sudden, though."

They headed into downtown, and the hum of the motor and the smooth motion of the car all conspired to make her feel very, very tired. She never had been able to stay awake inside a car for more than fifteen minutes, unless she was driving or in the middle of a conversation. And Daniel obviously wasn't feeling too talkative at the moment.

He put on his blinker and took an exit onto US 1, which seemed odd. She'd thought they were headed to his condo, which he'd told her was ten minutes from her studio. It might be a good idea to ask him where they were going, but her eyelids felt so heavy. Maybe she'd just close them for a minute and rest before she said anything.

She had no idea how much time had passed when she felt the car lurch to a stop.

"Whe-ah-wee?" she murmured, so exhausted she felt slightly drunk. She let her head fall toward Daniel, hoping that was enough to make him feel listened to.

"Watsonville."

Blinking her eyes rapidly to clear the sleep from them, she tried to focus on the building in front of them.

The building whose sign read, Erickson's Indoor Range and Gun Shop.

That woke her up in a hurry. "Oh, no. No, no, no, no, no."

"Adriana—"

She put her hand out in a stop gesture and waved it around, turning away from the windshield as if the mere sight of the building offended her. "I am a nonviolent person. I do not want to learn to shoot a gun." She dropped her hand and scanned the parking lot. "Is Liz here? Liz totally put you up to this, didn't she?"

Daniel definitely had the air of someone who hadn't expected her reaction. "She suggested that maybe—"

"Oh, there is no 'maybe' about it. I am not learning to shoot a gun. I hate guns."

The sunglasses came off again. Well, if he thought that his pretty eyes were enough to convince her to disrupt her lifelong practice of *ahimsa,* he had another think coming.

"Didn't you say you had a red belt in hapkido?" he asked.

"It's not the same thing. Martial arts is a very meditative practice, and you only strike in self-defense," she pointed out. "A gun's sole purpose in life is to blow a large hole into whatever ends up on the wrong side of it."

He just looked at her for a long moment, and even though she didn't mind looking back at him, it didn't make her want to budge on this. Guns accidentally discharged. Children found them and hurt themselves. If you didn't take care of them properly, they wouldn't even work when you needed them to.

"Adriana, you don't have to keep a gun in your house. You don't even have to keep one in my house, other than putting up with the ones I own," he said.

"Good. At least we agree on that."

"But I'm here to help you protect yourself," he continued. "And if Carter gets through me, I want to know that you could pick up my weapon and use it if you had to."

It felt like a slap in the face when he said that. She must have sounded like a petulant child to him. Here he was, putting his life on the line for her, and she couldn't even give him the reassurance that she could keep the two of them alive if it came down to it.

Or keep herself alive if Carter killed him.

"Daniel, you should just stay away from me," she said to the windshield. "I could leave the city, and you'd be—"

"Worried about you," he said. He reached out and touched her arm—just the barest brush of his fingers on her skin. It was enough to make her turn to him.

"Okay," she agreed. "I'll go."

They got out of the car and walked toward the nondescript gray building. How twisted was it that she'd always gravitated toward the hero types, the ones who not only put themselves in danger every day while on the job, but threw themselves bodily in its path whenever the option presented itself? She'd always thought the only person who could make her feel something, after James had died, would have to be someone in a nice, safe career, like an accountant or a pet groomer.

As they pushed through Erickson's glass double doors, the first thing she noticed was the incredible number of dead animals that graced the walls and shelves. A huge moose head hung over the main doors to what she assumed was the shooting range itself, staring down at them with its beady, glass eyes. Poor moose.

A long glass counter lined the entire far wall, behind which a tall, stocky man with dark hair and a goatee stood. He had on a dark green Erickson's T-shirt, with a name tag identifying him as Eric Owner. The unfortunately named Eric Erickson lifted a hand in greeting as they walked toward him.

"Hey, Danny Boy. How's life in the big city?"

"Not bad," Daniel replied, setting the small black case he'd carried in with him on the counter. He introduced Adriana, and then the two men engaged in some casual small talk while Eric unsnapped the case and took out Daniel's gun, checking the various components and bringing it up to his face to peer down the barrel.

"Could we get ten targets for the instructor bay and a box of range ammo?" Daniel said, laying his credit card on the counter. "All I have are hollow-points."

"Sure thing." He reached into a cabinet behind him and selected a small white box, which he smacked on the counter. "You shooting today, ma'am?"

"Yes." Reluctantly.

"Any possibility you could be pregnant?"

Daniel cleared his throat, and her own shock probably registered on her face, because Eric immediately qualified that statement. "Have to ask. Not safe for pregnant women in there."

"No. No chance," she said quickly, willing him to move on to the next topic.

"Okay, so here are the rules. Eye and ear protection must be worn whenever one of you is shooting." He pushed two pairs of red ear protectors and clear goggles toward them. "Shoot only at your target, one round per second—no rapid fire. Always keep firearms pointed down range and unloaded until ready to use. Do not lay a firearm down on the bench unless it's unloaded. No food, tobacco or beverages allowed. When you're finished, unload and case your firearm before leaving. When the command 'cease fire' is given, stop firing immediately and lay your gun down on the bench. Any questions?"

She wondered how many times a day he gave that particular monologue. He'd barely taken a breath while giving it. "No. I think I've got it."

"Great. Have a nice day, and enjoy your time on the range." He gestured toward the doors behind him. "See you, Danny."

They put on their ear protectors and goggles and went in, walking past ten numbered shooting bays until they arrived at another door at the end. Daniel opened it for her, and she saw that inside was a private shooting area.

"This is so I can talk to you in between shots," he said. "Otherwise we wouldn't be able to, wearing these things all the time." He tossed his ear protectors on the bench in front of them.

Daniel spent the first several minutes

teaching her how to load the ammo clip into the magazine, how to operate the safety and how to triangulate her body so the gun and her arms were situated protectively in front of her heart when she fired. Once he was sure she knew how to safely load, unload and prepare to fire, he finally said the words she'd been dreading.

"Now you're ready to shoot."

No, she really was not, but Daniel's words in the car made her keep quiet about it.

If Carter gets through me, I want to know you could pick up my gun and use it if you had to.

God, she hoped she never had to.

She had wondered if firing Daniel's Smith & Wesson was going to be similar to those scenes she'd seen in movies, where the guy gets behind the woman and puts his hands all over her in an effort to assist her stance. But she should have expected Daniel to be all business. He handed her the loaded gun, ensuring that she was pointing down range. A black-and-white paper target sat near the ceiling about twenty-five feet away from them.

"Grip it here," he said, showing her how his hand wrapped around the magazine. "Point your trigger finger along the barrel. You won't actually touch the trigger until you're good and ready to shoot." He handed her the gun.

Reluctantly, she curled her fingers around the magazine and pointed her other finger down the barrel.

"Bring your other hand up and rest the magazine in the middle of your palm." Instead of getting behind her and moving her body into position, he merely stood beside her and modeled his technique with an imaginary gun, so she could mimic him.

"It's a double-action semiautomatic," he told her. "When you fire the gun, it'll automatically reload. You don't have to cock it."

"Okay, whatever."

"So what you want to do is time your fire to your breathing. Basically, you breathe in—" his chest heaved as he inhaled deeply "—relax, squeeze the trigger when you're in your natural respiratory pause, then let go and exhale."

They practiced breathing together and pretending to fire the gun.

"Ready?"

She smirked at him. He stepped back, allowing her to approach the bench. She set the gun down and put on her goggles.

And then he laughed softly.

"What?" she asked, holding her ear protectors over her head.

"You look miserable."

She put the ear protectors down on the bench. "I'm fine."

His hazel eyes glinted with something that looked like amusement. Glad *he* found all of this funny. "You know, if you're not careful, Eric is probably going to come in here any second and tell you you're acting like a girl."

"Excuse me?"

He just smiled. Putting his ear protectors back on, he swept a hand toward the firing end of the bay.

She whirled on him as he leaned against the back wall and folded his arms. "Oh, no, no, no. You did *not* just say that to me."

Still grinning, he pointed at his fully covered ears and shrugged apologetically.

Fine. Okay. Breathe. She could do this.

She picked up the gun, pointing her trigger finger down the barrel and supporting the magazine with her other hand as he'd told her to. She narrowed her eyes, aiming the sights at the paper target. It was shaped like the silhouette of a man's upper torso, with a bull's-eye in the head and one over the heart.

Breathe. Relax.

Fire.

Exhale.

It took her a couple of shots to get her rhythm, especially with having to deal with the gun's recoil, but suddenly she was in a zone, and everything ceased to exist except the target, her hand and Daniel's gun.

Breathe. Relax. Fire. Breathe. Relax. Fire.

Exhale.

On her next shot, the gun didn't recoil. She checked to make sure it was out of ammo and set it down, barrel pointed down range. Pulling off her ear protectors, she felt Daniel approach behind her.

"Whoa," he breathed, looking over her shoulder. She was all too aware as his body brushed hers when he reached around her. He didn't seem to notice, too preoccupied with pushing the button that sent the target zipping toward them.

It clattered to a halt, the paper torso swinging forward with the momentum.

Three holes in the heart, two holes in the center of the forehead. And the rest had all hit the edges.

She tilted her head and looked sideways at him. His cheek nearly brushed hers as he checked out what she'd done. "Never shot a gun in your life, huh?"

She shook her head. "No."

He raised his dark eyebrows in admiration, putting his hands on her arms and squeezing them lightly. Encouragement. That's all he meant by it.

"I'd say you're a natural."

"I'd say I shoot like a girl," she deadpanned.

He laughed outright, as he moved away from her to lean against the wall again. "You do know I didn't mean that, right? I mean, the department makes us take gender-sensitivity training, and all."

Placing a finger on her cheek, she made a big show of pretending to consider what he'd just said. "So if I told Liz about that comment, you'd have to go through a refresher course, right?"

Daniel threw his hands up in surrender. "I'm sorry! I just wanted you to focus on something besides how much you didn't want to shoot that gun."

Men. "I'm a yoga instructor. I know how to breathe. The rest wasn't that hard."

His expression darkened as he crossed his arms, the Zen master all over again. "It is for some people."

She didn't know what he was thinking about, but it didn't seem like a pleasant topic. "So maybe we should go?"

He shook himself, pulling another clip off his holster, which was fully visible since he'd left his jacket in the car. "Actually I'd appreciate it if you'd do a few more targets. A couple of stationary and then I can get you some moving ones."

"I'd really like to go." She didn't know why, but suddenly the whole room seemed claustrophobic, and the last thing she wanted to do was touch that gun again. She didn't want to think about the reason she was learning to use it anymore. She just wanted to sleep.

"Addy, I'm not always going to be around to protect you," he said softly.

Her knees buckled. She slapped a palm against the cinder-block wall to right herself, hoping that he hadn't noticed.

But he had. In a flash he was standing directly beside her, his hands on her arms turning her to face him.

"You okay?"

It was something James had said to her. A lot. She hadn't known it then, but he'd been preparing her for the day she'd lose him.

She hadn't realized she'd clutched Daniel's

forearms, until her eyes focused again, and she saw her white-knuckled grasp. And though she knew she was acting ridiculous, she couldn't bring herself to let go.

"Daniel—"

As usual, he figured out what was going on in her head without her having to spell it out. "You've heard that before, haven't you?"

She didn't respond. She didn't have to.

He pulled her into his arms again. And she let him, resting her cheek against the soft fabric of his dress shirt, feeling the lean muscles of his chest underneath and remembering what it had felt like to be held and loved.

"I promise you," he murmured into her hair, "as long as it doesn't drive you crazy to have someone like me shadowing your every move, I'm here. Nothing's going to happen to you."

She pulled back, but he refused to let her go completely. "To either of us," he added.

"You can't promise that," she said to her hands.

Out of the corner of her eye, she saw him look away. "No. You're right, I can't."

Chapter Nine

They spent the next several days in Daniel's condo, though things had grown quieter between them since the day at the shooting range. He always treated her with a polite respectfulness, but there was a distance between them. And she knew it had everything to do with James, even though neither one of them had brought him up since she'd moved in.

But when they did talk, they always fell into easy conversation, carefully dancing around both James and the growing attraction between them. She knew it was there—she could feel it every time she looked at him, every time she accidentally touched him. And sometimes, when she caught him off guard, she could see something in his green-and-gold eyes that looked like he just might want her back.

They never talked about it, though. There just weren't words.

By the middle of the week, she could tell that Daniel was going a little stir-crazy being cooped up at home and receiving reports on the investigation via phone. So she wasn't at all surprised when she got up one morning to find Liz reclining on the tan U-shaped hi-I'm-a-bachelor couch in the middle of Daniel's living room.

Liz used the remote she was holding to switch the set off, then sat up to smooth the fabric of her dark trousers. "Well, hey, Addy."

Daniel rose from the other end of the couch as Addy walked into the room.

Adriana narrowed her eyes at her friend. "So what's up? You're on the clock, so I'm guessing something's happened."

"Not exactly." She tossed the remote back on the couch with a soft thump. "Take it away, Cardenas."

That's when she noticed he was back in a suit, instead of the jeans and sweatshirts he'd been wearing around the condo. "I'm going back to the Sanchez scene. Liz is going to stay with you for a while."

"Well, that was delicate." Liz arched an eyebrow at him before turning back to Addy. "We think you two might have been on to something, with the poem," she explained.

"But we haven't been able to find what Daniel says we should be looking for, back at the Sanchez crime scene. So Daniel's going to check it out, since he's the only one of us who has any idea what iambic heptameter is. We thought he might be able to find something that the rest of us missed."

It wasn't being left alone with Liz that bothered her. Liz was more than a capable cop and an excellent markswoman, too, if it came down to that. But it was about Daniel. A fear she knew was irrational grabbed hold of her, and she couldn't do anything to stop it from seeping into her mind, whispering in her ear exactly what she was afraid of. Daniel, alone in that house, where Elijah Carter might have been. Maybe Carter liked to come back to his killing fields. Maybe he would be there, waiting....

Something on her face must've tipped Liz off, because she straightened suddenly and got up to amble toward the kitchen. "Got anything to eat, Cardenas? I'm starving." She didn't bother to wait for Daniel's response—Addy could hear her rummaging around in the kitchen, banging cupboards and stomping around in a not-so-subtle attempt at giving them privacy.

Daniel's mouth twisted into something between a grin and a grimace, as if he didn't know whether to laugh or be annoyed. "What was that?" he asked.

"I don't—" She couldn't even speak, so instead she just moved in front of him. Before she could stop herself, her hands reached out to clutch the lapels of his suit jacket. She should have known he was planning on going back out on the job again—why else would he have put his tie back on? "I just—"

"What is it?"

She clung to his jacket for all she was worth, as if she could anchor him to the spot. "Don't go," she said quietly. And then the air between them suddenly became charged. She could hear him breathing, feel his heartbeat beneath her hands, feel her own, threatening to burst through her chest. She stared at the subtle pattern on the blue silk of his tie until it blurred, until she couldn't breathe.

"Adriana," he murmured. God, she loved the way he said her name. "Beautiful girl." He pulled her into his arms, against his broad, muscular body, and she let him hold her up, because she didn't think she could stand on her own anymore. Her head fit perfectly in the space between his collarbone and shoulder, and she could see a pulse beating steadily under the brown skin of his neck.

She wanted to lean forward and taste him there, wanted to plunge her hands in his hair and curl her legs around his lean hips, daring him to finish everything unspoken between them, everything they'd started. She slipped her hand underneath his jacket and grabbed a fistful of fabric, wanting to tear at his shirt. Wanting to find his bed and pin him to it, kiss that full, gorgeous mouth until they couldn't breathe, until she made him crazy. She wanted him, right here, right now, needed to anchor him to this space in the most primal way possible. She barely cared that Liz was in the next room. "Don't go," she whispered urgently against his skin, her lips brushing his throat.

A low groan rumbled inside his chest, and she loved that she could affect him that way. "Addy, you need to think about what you're doing," he whispered. He dipped his head to plant a gentle kiss on her jawline, making her feel as if she'd gone liquid in his arms.

Think. Who needed to think? She tilted her head, her eyelids heavy as she sought out his perfect mouth. She touched her lips to his, and for a moment, they remained frozen like that. He was holding back, and she hated it. Slipping her fingers into his dark hair, she tugged his head down. *"Oye, Papi,"* she murmured against his mouth. *"Ven aqui."*

When he still didn't move, her eyes flew open. And she watched a slow, incredibly sexy grin spread across his handsome face.

"Come here, hey?" he murmured, his green-and-gold eyes locked on to hers as if they were the only two people in the world. With a glance at the doorway through which Liz had disappeared earlier, he advanced on her, guiding her backward into a hallway well out of Liz's line of sight. And then…

Then he was finally, finally kissing her, his mouth teasing at first. He took her bottom lip gently between his teeth, then let go, and she hungrily rose up on her toes so he wouldn't stop. "You're beautiful," he murmured against her mouth, and then they were kissing again, hungrily, deeply. She felt her back hit the wall as he pinned her against it, and she reached down and yanked at his shirt until it came free of his pants, and she could slip her hands underneath. She ran her palms up his back, loving the feel of his smooth skin, of the muscles bunching and pulling underneath. After nearly a week of dancing around each other, this had been a long time coming.

Just as she'd nearly forgotten Liz had ever existed, Daniel pulled back, bracing himself with a forearm against the wall as his chest heaved up and down with each ragged breath.

"*Me hace loco,*" he murmured.

You make me crazy. She loved that she could do that. It had been a long time since someone had said that to her.

James. The name hit her like a bucket of ice water. James had said that to her.

And he'd died.

As if he'd read her mind, Daniel pulled back out of her reach, his angular features carefully schooled into that cool, unreadable Zen master expression he adopted when he was working.

"Daniel," she said, hating the pleading tone in her voice. She didn't know what she wanted. She didn't know what to say to him. That he took her breath away? That he made her feel things she'd never thought she'd feel again? That she hated, really hated, the fact that he was a cop? That he frightened her more than words could express?

He tucked his shirt back in without looking at her, carefully arranged his tie. But then his eyes met hers, and his expression softened into the Daniel she knew. Was getting to know.

"I meant what I said. You do need to think about what you're doing," he said. He stepped toward her, brushed the softest of kisses across her cheek. "Because I stop thinking whenever I'm around you, Adriana."

His touch was so tender, it almost made her cry. She let her palms rest against his chest again, but whether it was because she had to touch him or to push him away, she didn't know.

She was so messed up. So pathetically, completely messed up. Why in the world did Daniel Cardenas have to be a cop?

"I'm not sure what just happened there, but I do know there are some ghosts standing between us," he said gently, reaching up to finger the piece of silk tying back her hair. "And even with this red scarf in your hair, Adriana, you're still wearing mostly black."

He straightened. She loosened her hold on him. And he let her go. "Think about it, Adriana. This is all your decision." His eyes fairly glowed—a dark, dangerous look. "Because I know exactly what I want."

Think. She had to think. He was right—she wasn't ready for this. He was going to go, back to that house, and only God knew if he'd come back to her again. "Don't go," she said again.

"I'll be back, Adriana," he replied. "I promise."

"I'm sorry," she said, feeling suddenly ridiculous. She clasped her hands together under her chin, squeezing her fingers so hard she knew she was probably cutting off all circulation to them. "I don't want to be one of those miserable, clingy people. It's just…I feel as if you're safe as long as I can see you."

He just looked at her, until they both heard Liz clear her throat and walk noisily back into the room. "I know." And she knew they were both thinking of James.

ASIDE FROM THE OBVIOUS reasons, leaving Adriana when she was feeling vulnerable was the last thing Daniel wanted to do. But he couldn't hide the reality of his job from her, either. This was what he did, day after day, week after week. Just like her last boyfriend.

Like he was her boyfriend just because they'd gone at each other like that for a few minutes. A few really great, really incredible minutes.

Grip. He seriously needed to get one. Now.

Get a grip and stop thinking about her. Because she made it clear that she was still thinking about someone else. Sure, he could get under her skin if he got all up in her face about it, but…

There was a fine line between being assertive and being Stan—especially when it came to Adriana and what she'd been through with Brentwood. Whatever happened between them had to be her decision. And God help him, something did seem to be happening between them.

Pulling his car up in front of Janie Sanchez's house, Daniel got out of the car with his evidence kit, pushing all thoughts of Adriana, her deceased fiancé and the way her amazing mouth moved against his out of his head.

As much as he could, anyway.

He ducked under the crime-scene tape that still cordoned off the small bungalow's front yard, making his way up to the front steps.

The rest of the neighborhood was quiet for a Saturday—no one tending their yards, no kids running around. He didn't suppose he'd feel like barbecuing, either, if a young woman had been tortured and killed next door.

Using the keys Liz had given him, he let

himself in, crouching under more yellow tape that crisscrossed the doorway.

Dropping the rectangular case that held his portable evidence kit on the ground with a loud thud, he took in his surroundings. The cops on the scene had drawn the curtains to prevent the neighbors from seeing inside, and they were still drawn. So even though it was late morning and sunny outside, the light inside of the house was dim, hazy.

A few stray beams of sunlight shot past gaps in the curtains, dust particles floating lazily inside them. A thin film of dust already coated every smooth surface.

He walked slowly through the front sitting room, his footsteps echoing on the hardwood floor. The house was still an active crime scene, so the MPD hadn't yet allowed the owners to call in a cleanup crew. Everything was just as they'd left it the night Janie had been murdered. The story was still here, for anyone who wanted to read it….

Someone had picked the lock—a hack job, judging by the scrapes beside the doorknob. Janie and her roommate had had a chain lock as a backup, but whoever had jimmied their door lock had come prepared. Bolt cutters, from the looks of it, had neatly severed the thin chain in two.

He wasn't a blood-spatter expert, but the spray of medium-size droplets on the wall to the right of him seemed to indicate that Janie had been subjected to blunt-force trauma. Elijah Carter had always liked to quickly subdue his victims, either through a surprise blitz attack, or by drugging them with a rag soaked in chloroform. And then he'd tie them up and torture them once they couldn't fight back.

He pressed the wall switch for some extra light, not wanting to open the curtains to prying neighbors. Nothing happened.

Right. Power had been cut.

Some people might have thought it was odd—that a man as strong as Carter would feel the need to sneak up on his victims. But it made a strange kind of sense. Carter had been special forces in the military until he'd been dishonorably discharged. And the military would have trained him to use the element of surprise to his advantage to achieve his objective. As a soldier that objective would have been to disarm an enemy combatant as quickly as possible, to prevent harm to yourself and others. For Elijah

Carter, the objective would be to gain total control over his victim as quickly as possible. Because Elijah Carter thrived on total control. Controlling fear by stalking and terrorizing his intended victims. Controlling his victim's body by tying her down and inflicting pain. Controlling life and death by strangling and reviving her, again and again and again.

God, Janie Sanchez was just a kid.

Detach, Cardenas. Keep moving.

Taking a small metal flashlight off his gun belt, he shone it around the room. Other than the dust that had settled in the past few days, it was clean. The walls had been painted a sunny yellow, and Janie and her roommate, both students, had decorated with inexpensive pine wood and wicker chairs and end tables. The one nicer piece of furniture was the oval mahogany coffee table that sat in the center of the space. A huge ding on one dark-stained leg gave him the impression that they might have gotten a good deal on it secondhand. A glass vase full of more pink and white carnations than he'd ever seen in one spot sat in the middle of the table. The stems on most of the flowers were bent, and the petals were all edged with brown, the water in the vase murky.

He'd been about to head for the next room, but instead, on a hunch, he walked around the table.

On the other side of the vase, someone had written LOOK in the dust coating the table's surface.

That had definitely not been there the night Janie Sanchez had died.

Okay, look for what? He checked under the table and rechecked the entire room. But nothing jumped out at him as being out of the ordinary.

He went into the next room, the living room where they'd found Janie's body. A massive bloodstain, now dried, still coated a good portion of the floor, matching the one on her mattress where she'd actually been murdered. He'd expected to see that.

What he hadn't expected was the sheet of paper lying smack in the middle of it. It wasn't in any way soaked with blood, so someone had obviously put it there after Janie's blood had dried.

He listened for a moment, just in case, but the house was as still and silent as if no one had lived there for a hundred years. Yanking a pair of latex gloves out of his pocket, he put them on as he moved to check out the paper.

Two lines had been printed on it, using an obsolete dot-matrix printer.

You tell me, twisted, impure girl,
why it was you lured me in?
Take her eyes, cut out her heart.
And taste the blood on her sweet skin.

Adriana had been right. The son of a bitch thought he was a poet.

He reread the lines, the damn meter sticking in his head like a bad commercial jingle.

Janie Sanchez still had her eyes and her heart when they'd found her. What the hell did this mean?

Gloves on, he picked up a small silver button left on top of the note, presumably to hold it in place. He turned it over and saw it was a refrigerator magnet.

Still holding both the note and the magnet, he rose, heading into the kitchen. More blood spatter here, on the apple-green walls, and flecking the legs of the cheap pine table and chairs. Janie may have run toward the back of the house, only to be pursued into and ultimately subdued in this room.

Detach.

As he walked up to the ancient, avocado-green refrigerator, he noticed that more of the silver button magnets dotted its doors. Glancing at the one in his gloved hand, he confirmed that they were the same.

Subtle. Someone would have to look at the crime-scene photographs to make sure, but the note probably had been stuck to the fridge when they'd been investigating the scene. And since they'd missed the note the first time around, someone had come back into the house to relocate it to a place where no one would ever miss it.

The rhythm was similar to the other lines on the Internet—and it seemed to continue the poem, just as Addy had said. Though it might not have held up in court, to Daniel, the new "verse" was a critical piece of a puzzle that up until now hadn't been too coherent.

Whether the perp knew it or not, it had been smart to use a dot-matrix. Most laser printer manufacturers had quietly modified their machines so they encoded the serial number and manufacturing code on every printout. The code of yellow dots was impossible to see with the naked eye. Look at the page through a blue filter or with a blue LED light, and that changed. Meaning they could have traced the paper to the printer beyond the shadow of a doubt.

With an ancient dot-matrix printer, or even a newer ink-jet printer, they were out of luck in that respect. But what he held in his hand was still important. It was proof that the Web site wasn't just a jacked-up prank—it was real. It linked Janie's murderer with whoever had set up the site. And it was a warning…of what someone was planning to do to Adriana if he ever got her alone.

Of course, he'd have to go through Daniel first.

Chapter Ten

"So, what's going on with you and my partner?"

Leave it to Liz to be that direct about something Addy wasn't even sure of. She grabbed the television remote and spent more time than necessary trying to figure out how to turn down the volume on Daniel's gigantic TV.

The two of them had spent the better part of the afternoon slouched in the corners of the U-shaped couch, which wasn't much to look at but felt incredibly soft when you sat in it. They'd watched TV and had avoided more difficult subjects, for lack of a better way to put it. But when Addy had asked for the fifth time if they should call Daniel to make sure he was all right, apparently the cop had decided that the gloves were coming off.

"Oh, gimme that thing." Liz stretched over to where Addy was sitting and snatched the remote out of her hands. She quickly punched the mute button, then turned her level gaze onto Addy. "Not that it's any of my business, but I'll ask again, anyway, because you expect me to. What is going on with you and my partner?" Her tone was an interesting combination of maternal instinct and bossy detective.

Addy shrugged sheepishly. "Nothing?"

"If it were really nothing, you wouldn't have said that as if it was a question." Tossing the remote down on the couch, Liz slid across the enormous couch closer to her. Addy slid away as far as she could, until she hit the corner. She knew an interrogation technique when she saw it.

Sure enough, Liz went right for the kill. "And those slurping noises I heard when you two disappeared meant what? He decided inhaling you would be the best way to protect you?"

Grabbing a boring brown throw pillow, Adriana threw it two-handed at Liz's head. It was easily deflected. "Nice. What are you, twelve?"

"Twelve and a half." Even though she'd just told a joke—a lame one, but still a joke—Liz's expression grew somber, even a little sad, the way it always did when she was about to deliver a "poor, pathetic Addy" talk.

"Seriously," Liz continued, "I just wanted you to know that he is a really great guy. Perfect gentleman, hell of a detective and one of the most honorable people I know." She paused to consider that statement. "If you can get him to talk, that is. You know, that whole Zen master thing he's got going on."

Which reminded Addy of something. "What about the Kama Sutra master?"

"Oh, God, you met her?" Liz wrinkled her freckled nose in disgust, obviously thinking about Daniel's flashy ex-girlfriend. "Oh, right, at the annual ball that one year. She was awful."

"Just very loud." As much as she hated to admit it, Adriana felt retroactively jealous. Which was idiotic. She'd gone to that ball with James, had hardly noticed Cardenas at the time except in the way you always noticed a ridiculously good-looking guy for a few seconds when he walked into your line of vision.

"So, okay, at one time he had terrible taste in women," Liz admitted. "But if I remember correctly, he didn't go out with her for that long. He's not a womanizer." Slouching back into the cushions, she propped her feet up on the ottoman squatting in front of them. "Believe me, I'd know. I wake him up all the time because of work."

Addy slouched alongside her. "He does seem like a great guy."

"He is."

"But you know what drives me nuts?" Addy asked. "He has two expressions—broody and more broody. Oh, and then there's I'm-smoking-hot-and-I'm-going-to-kiss-you."

"Right." Liz grimaced. "I'm getting a little creeped out by this conversation. He's like my brother…."

Whatever their relationship, Addy doubted that Daniel saw much of this Liz—the sarcastic, fun Liz for whom no topic was too personal. She wondered if Daniel had this side to him, or if he was always so serious. She'd seen a glimpse of a looser, freer Daniel on rare occasions, but would he ever be able to let his guard down around her fully? Or would he always be worried about her past, wondering about James?

Of course, she had to let the past go if she wanted Daniel to do the same.

"Isn't it time to put all the black away?" Liz asked. "You've been sad for so long, Addy. I'd love to see you happy again."

She looked down before saying quietly, "Tomorrow is his birthday."

That statement landed like a thud in the middle of the room, bringing the conversation to a screeching halt, as she'd known it would. She didn't have to tell Liz whose birthday it was.

"I didn't remember," Liz replied.

"I do. Every year."

Her friend shifted so she was facing Addy, instead of the TV. "I wish you could—"

Get over it. Get past this. Accept that he's gone. James would want you to be happy. James would want you to go on. She'd heard it all so many times, she could give herself a pep talk faster than anyone else could. Unfortunately, words never made her actually get over her fiancé having been murdered by a psychopath.

But then Liz slumped back against the cushions. "God, I wish I could just stop missing him. But we can't, can we?" she said softly. "And he was just my friend, not someone I loved the way you did."

A tear rolled down Addy's cheek, and she swiped it quickly away with the back of her hand. "Nope, we can't," she said, proud of how steady her voice had been, even as her vision blurred. The two women remained silent for a moment, lost in their shared grief. It was a strange bond to have with someone, but she was grateful for Liz all the same.

"I usually go to the cemetery, but I think it will be too dangerous," Addy said to the television. "Anyway, I don't want Daniel to know."

"Okay."

They sat there in silence, before Liz spoke again. "Did I hear you right? Did you actually call him *papi?*"

Addy couldn't help herself—she laughed. "Yes."

"Doesn't that mean Daddy? Because *eeeuuw.*"

She almost wished she had another pillow to throw. "Technically speaking, yes, but it's not like that in Spanish. When you call the man you're with Papi, you're just basically telling him he's hot."

Liz raised a skeptical eyebrow.

"I'm serious," Addy said. "It's not gross in my language. I so totally wouldn't call a guy Daddy in English."

After some good-natured ribbing about the whole *papi* thing, Liz decided to get up and get a glass of water. She offered to get one for Addy, who gratefully accepted.

With some difficulty, Addy also hefted herself out of the plush cushions that had conformed to her body like a giant sponge, searching for the TV remote. Just then, a loud thump, like a knock, sounded from outside, near the door.

"Liz?" she called. But she heard water running in the kitchen sink, pinging so loudly off the stainless steel, she was sure Liz hadn't heard her.

Slowly and quietly as she could, she crept in her stocking feet toward the door. At least she could see who it was before she screamed for the woman with the gun. Placing her hands slowly and carefully against the steel panel, she peered through the peephole.

It was a teenage boy—about sixteen or seventeen, she guessed. Vintage Pogues T-shirt, baggy pants, flannel tied around the waist, chin-length blond surfer hair.

That would be the same teenager she sometimes saw in *her* neighborhood, that she and Daniel had seen just a few days ago skateboarding in the street.

What the heck was he doing here, across town?

He started to walk down the path to the street, and without really stopping to think about what she was doing, she unlocked the door and yanked it open.

"Hey!" she called. "Did you just knock?"

Startled, he turned around, his eyes darting from side to side as he considered his options. Then he seemed to focus on something just over her left shoulder. She turned.

A serrated hunting knife was impaled in the siding of Daniel's condo. She didn't have to be a rocket scientist to know that another macabre message was stuck to it.

A hot flush washed over her body, and her vision narrowed until all she could see was that knife. How dare he. How dare he do this to her. How dare he make everything that had happened, everything she'd lost, into some kind of horrible joke.

Yanking the knife free, she advanced on the boy, who stood rooted to the spot, looking as if he'd bolt at any second. Somewhere in the back of her mind, she wondered why he didn't. He could easily outrun her.

"What is the *matter* with you?" she shouted, so angry she could barely form a coherent sentence. "Why would you *do* this?"

"I didn't—" He held his hands up and shrank away as she shook the blade at him. He didn't look psycho—he looked like a normal teenager who'd just pulled a prank and was afraid she'd call the cops. Guess he hadn't checked to see whose house this was.

"Do you think this is *funny* or something? Do you all have a good laugh at my expense every Halloween, while I'm missing the man I loved more than anything?" She barely registered the fact that a car had pulled into Daniel's driveway. Behind her, she could hear Liz shouting, but she didn't care. "You stupid, nasty little creep."

"Hey, stop jabbing that thing in my face," the kid said, throwing his palms in the air and backing away from her.

"Addy, no!" she heard Liz shout.

A car door slammed. "Adriana!"

Daniel's voice.

Don't you dare hurt him.

All of her anger focused on the kid, and when he reached for the knife, to try to take it away from her, she was ready for him. His hand closed around her wrist. She dropped the knife, twisted her hand up and around. Pushing down on the back of his wrist, she swung her body under his arm and yanked the arm upward. He cried out, his elbow pointed awkwardly in the air. She still had a hold of his hand with one hand, twisting it painfully along with the rest of his arm. Every time he tried to struggle, she twisted his arm more, causing him enough pain that he soon gave up. She pulled her free arm back, aiming at the pinky side of his hand with the heel of her own.

"Move again, and I will break the hell out of your arm," she snarled. The little twerp obviously hadn't been expecting her to know how to fight back.

Before she knew what was happening, Liz was at her side, pulling her away as Daniel grabbed the kid and handcuffed his hands behind his back.

"What are you doing? She attacked me," the kid shouted, his hair falling into his eyes as Daniel finished fastening the cuffs. Fortunately for him, he didn't struggle.

"Right," he said calmly, though there was an edge to his voice that she hadn't heard before. "There's a knife on the ground and a chunk of siding taken out of my house. And I've seen you before on Mermaid Point. Not too hard to put that all together."

Taking the guy by the arm, Daniel led him to his car. He opened the back door and guided the kid in by pushing down on the top of his head.

Daniel turned back around, stalking toward the spot where Adriana stood and looking angrier than she'd ever seen him. When he finally stood before her, she could hear him breathing hard, his eyes smoldering as he looked down at her. "What," he ground out, "the hell did you think you were doing?"

"I didn't think. I just…acted." She looked him in the eye as she explained her actions. Looking back on it, coming out bare-handed to greet a perfect stranger who had minutes before been holding a knife hadn't been one of her finest moments. But she'd been cooped up inside hiding from a deranged killer for days—had been hiding for four years, truth be told—and she'd thought that Daniel, of all people, would have understood that she'd finally just snapped.

His jaw worked for a moment. "I'll talk to you later," he said, his voice low and soft and all the more dangerous for it. He opened his mouth as if to say something and then shook his head, turning away from her. She watched him walk to his car, get in and drive off.

A FEW HOURS LATER, the phone rang in Daniel's condo, and Liz picked it up. She spoke to the caller for a couple of minutes, then hung up.

"Daniel wants us to meet him at the station."

Adriana had been in the kitchen, trying to figure out how to make a chai latte with Daniel's gigantic espresso machine. She sighed. "I'm not really looking forward to that. He seems pretty upset with me."

Having left most of her stuff in one spot on the kitchen counter, Liz grabbed her gun belt and strapped it on over her white button-down shirt. "Yeah, you know, I've seen Cardenas emote more during the last few days than I have in his entire four years with the Homicide Department. What's up with that?"

With a spray and a hiss, the machine steamed her chai, causing it to foam at the top. She removed the little metal pitcher from under the steam wand and poured the contents into a waiting travel mug. "I don't know."

"I do. But you two can figure it out. I've got more important things to deal with." Snapping her gun in place, Liz dragged her keys across the granite and pocketed them. "And that was pretty stupid, going out there without some kind of protection. Like, oh, *me.*"

Addy felt all the tension in her body settle at the base of her neck, and her shoulders drooped slightly. "It was. I'll be more careful next time."

"Not that I blame you. Stupid little punk." Liz's mouth twisted in disgust. "He lawyered up. Daniel just told me he couldn't get a thing out of him."

Now, that sucked. The piece of paper he'd impaled on Daniel's home had been blank—not another verse to the poem they'd expected. And the knife was one of the cheap butcher knives that had been appearing at her door every Halloween. "Who put him up to it?"

"He claims it was just a Halloween prank." She snorted, shoving her hands in the pockets of her midlength navy blue coat. "Says he meant to get a friend, and accidentally stabbed a cop's house."

"Oh, come on." They headed for the front door, stopping at the hall closet so Adriana could get her own coat and purse out.

"I know!" Liz locked the door behind them, and they headed down the front walkway to her car. "If that kind of coincidence is happening to you, maybe we should stop and get you a lottery ticket."

It took them less than ten minutes to get to the police station, and Daniel was waiting for them in the parking lot, leaning against his off-duty Dodge Charger with his arms folded and his damned mirrored sunglasses on his face. He didn't speak to her as she got out of Liz's car and approached him. And when she finally stood directly in front of him, he just moved around to the passenger side and opened the door for her, stony-faced. She got in, giving him a questioning look as she did so. But he didn't respond.

She heard him say goodbye to Liz, and then he got in, starting the engine without saying a word.

When they'd been on the road for a little while, she finally couldn't stand it anymore. "Daniel—"

"I'm sorry," he said.

The interruption couldn't have shocked her more. "For what?"

"If I'd been through everything you have, I might have done the same thing and gone after that kid, too." He still didn't look at her, keeping his eyes on the road. The tightness in his jaw and shoulders told her he was still grappling with anger or some other strong emotion. "I had no right to shout at you."

"That was shouting?" She almost laughed. "Daniel, you barely spoke above a whisper. Although I have to say, you're still pretty scary when you're quiet."

"I was angry." He turned to face her for a

long moment, then turned his focus back on the road. "When I saw you, out there taking on a guy twice your size, without a single weapon…" He paused. "It made me wonder if you have some sort of death wish."

Death wish. As in she wanted to die, to get back to James. "I— Of course not. I told you, I just snapped. I have no desire to off myself anytime soon—and yes, I would do it, if I felt that way, rather than let some punk kid do it for me."

With a curt nod that let her know he was finished with the subject if she was, he glanced over his shoulder. When she looked behind them, she saw a couple of full grocery bags sitting in the backseat. "There's something I've been putting off since you…since I brought you home. Mind coming with me?" he asked softly.

Mind? After he'd turned his life upside down and let her invade his space 24/7 to keep her safe? "Not at all."

They drove in silence, eventually hitting Seventeen Mile Drive, which hugged the Monterey Peninsula's rocky coastline and offered spectacular views of the Pacific. At one point the car took a curve along a low, jutting cliff, and down below, Adriana could see a herd of seals lounging along the shore. A few miles later Daniel pulled off onto a side road that led to a large manor-style building. The sign near the driveway read "Carmel Valley Terrace: a Life Care Living Center."

"My father lives here." Daniel pulled into a spot that was as close as he could get to the large oak front doors without a disabled sticker. "I'm sorry I have to bring you here, but I visit him every week."

"It's okay. I'm glad you asked me to come."

His mouth curved upward in a smile that looked sad, even though she couldn't see his eyes behind his glasses. He got out of the car, taking the paper sacks out of the back.

She walked beside him up the brick-lined path flanked by low, rounded sand verbena plants, the pink and white clustered flowers in full bloom. The thick green leaves brushed their legs as they walked.

"I have to warn you," he said just before they reached the front door, "Dad has dementia. It can make him a little...unpredictable."

There was nothing she could say to that that didn't sound ridiculous, so she just settled for, "That must be really hard on you."

"I'm getting used to it." He started to reach for the door handle, but she pulled it open for him first, since he was carrying stuff. "I should come more often, but…"

The doors opened up to a huge, beautifully furnished room that was almost all windows. Through the far bank, a sweeping, clay-tiled courtyard was visible, dotted with ironwork benches and tables, and clusters of flowering plants in full bloom.

A receptionist seated at a mahogany desk greeted Daniel by name, and he headed for a door at the far end.

Unlike the dry, sterile nursing homes she'd been to, the Carmel Valley Terrace looked more like a plush, exclusive resort. It must have cost a fortune.

They headed down a hallway to room 221, and Daniel rapped his knuckles on the door before he twisted the knob.

A man Adriana estimated to be in his seventies sat in a beige recliner, watching television. He had a full shock of steel-gray hair that stood up on end and a scowl on his face nearly identical to the one she'd seen on Daniel's after he'd handcuffed that teenager. Daniel set the bags on the counter of the small kitchenette at the far end of the large room, then came back and kissed his father on the forehead. "Hey, Dad. How you doing?"

Mr. Cardenas waved him away with an impatient flap of his hand. "I told you, I don't want any more of that poison you call medicine," he said hoarsely, with the accent of a native Spanish speaker. "I just want to watch my show." He craned his neck, trying to see around the two of them. Addy sidestepped out of his line of vision.

"I'm not a nurse, Dad. I'm your son." Taking a chair from the small dining set in the corner, Daniel set it down near Addy, then pulled one next to his father for himself.

"My son? Ruben?"

Daniel didn't respond right away. He bowed his head, examining his hands, his expression carefully neutral. *"No, soy Daniel, Papi."* He gestured toward Adriana, almost as if he were trying to beat his father's reaction to his identity. *"Y esta es Adriana Torres.* Adriana, Ruben Cardenas."

"Daniel." He practically spit out the name. "That is one good-for-nothing boy. Can't even watch his brother when I ask him to. Can't count on him for anything."

Thinking of her own warmhearted parents, who never had an unkind word for anyone, much less their own daughter, Adriana couldn't even speak. Dementia or no, who would say that about his own son? Who would say that about *Daniel?*

"Now, Ruben." With a grunt, Ruben, Sr., shifted in his chair to face Adriana. "That's a real man. Did you know my Ruben is a cop? Just like his old man, but better. Youngest detective on the force."

With a feeble attempt at an answering smile, she glanced at Daniel, who sat stone-faced next to his father. Sometimes he'd pat his father on the back or the arm, but mostly he just looked out the window at the gardens, as if trying to ignore the hateful things the man was saying.

"Daniel loves you, Mr. Cardenas. He brought you some snacks and things you like and put them in the kitchen." She guessed what had been in the paper bags Daniel had carried in.

"Oh, no. That's Ruben. My Ruben comes to see me every week."

She wasn't about to yell at a man with dementia, but if this was the way he'd treated Daniel all throughout his childhood, she wasn't sure the man deserved weekly treats and a room in the Trump Towers of nursing homes. She opened her mouth to correct Mr. Cardenas, when she caught Daniel's eye.

Almost imperceptibly he shook his head, his eyes telling her everything. "He must love you very much," she choked out instead.

The rest of their brief visit went pretty much the same. Daniel made his dad some decaffeinated *café con leche,* and the man insisted on calling him Ruben all the time. Apparently, Ruben was just a few weeks short of being canonized and voted President.

Finally, Daniel stood, and Adriana was only too happy to leave the sad scene behind. "Is there anything else I can get you, Papi?" he asked.

"No, no." Taking his eyes off the television, the older man regarded his son. "You're a good boy. You take care of your father. Is your mother coming home soon?"

Daniel didn't respond to the last question, embracing his father instead.

Turning his green-and-gold eyes on Adriana, Mr. Cardenas held out a soft, knobby hand. She shook it gently. "It was nice to meet you, Mr. Cardenas. You have two very nice sons."

With a hmph, the older man sat back in his chair, contemplating his television once more.

She left Daniel alone while they made their way off the grounds and back to the car.

They'd gone halfway back to Daniel's condo when he finally spoke.

"He wasn't always like that. He was a great father, before his mind started to go."

"I'm glad," she said.

He started to lift his sunglasses out of his pocket, then released his hold on them with a sigh. "Ruben was older than I was. He died ten years ago. Papi never quite got over it."

"Oh, God, Daniel." She'd had no idea. Here she'd been going on and on about losing James, and she'd never stopped to wonder if Daniel had ever lost someone important to him, too. "I'm so sorry."

He gave her a sad smile. "What my father said was true. He was a cop. The Cardenas boys bleed blue, Papi always said." Resting one arm on the ledge between the door and the window, he glanced out at the ocean spreading out like a sheet of deep-blue glass below them. "Ruben was killed off duty when a gang member found out where he lived and shot him. He should have been in prison, based on all the drug-related evidence Ruben had gathered against him. But the combination of an incompetent district attorney and a too-lenient judge resulted in that scum going back on the streets. And my brother died because of it." He raked a hand through his hair, causing it to spike up even more than it already did.

"Was he angry at you, because you were the one left behind?" She knew she was prying, but somehow she knew it was okay. Opening up wasn't exactly Daniel's style. If he was talking to her about his past, it was because he felt it was important that she know.

He blew out a long, slow breath. "Nah. Papi and Ruben had more in common—Ruben loved baseball and football, whereas I liked track and computers." He laughed, staring at the road as if his past were written there. "My brother was so outgoing. There was this crabby old lady who lived across from us, used to actually shake her fist at us whenever we rode our bikes by her house. She scared me, but one day, Ruben goes over there and offers to, I don't know, water her plants or something. And suddenly she's baking us cookies and can't say enough about how nice we are."

Suddenly the corners of his mouth tightened, and he jerked his head, as if trying to shake off strong emotions. "I was the quiet one."

Adriana took his hand, holding it tightly in both of hers. "You don't say?"

"Hard to believe, hey?" He squeezed her hand. "The doctor says Papi conflates the two of us. He's angry that Ruben is gone, so he's blended us both into one superson, and evil Daniel is the boy who left him."

Tracing a finger along the veins in the back of his hand, Adriana murmured, "It'd be nice if the superson was named after the one who's still alive."

He glanced down at their hands, then directed his concentration back on the winding road. "Sure it would. But his mind is broken, and I have to remember that. I never felt he didn't love me or loved Ruben more, when he wasn't sick. I can't start feeling that way now."

When they finally reached Daniel's condo, Adriana wrapped her arms around him as soon as they were out of the car. "I hate that this happened to your family," she said, as he clung to her, his hands tangling in her hair.

They stood like that for a moment, and then she felt him take a deep, shuddering breath. He pulled back, looking her straight in the eye. "I just wanted to tell you…I know what it's like to live with ghosts." Stepping out of her arms, he reached out and took one of her hands, bringing it up to his lips. Just that soft contact of his mouth on her skin made her breathless.

"But I can only handle coming in second best for one person in my life, and that's my father."

Chapter Eleven

Adriana.

She stirred, her head thick and ponderous from sleep. It wrapped around her like a perfumed cloud, catching her limbs and making them heavy, so heavy. She'd just turn her head, close her eyes, and she'd be unconscious again….

Adriana, it whispered again.

She knew that voice.

Opening her eyes, she saw she was standing in the middle of a wooded park, the trees impossibly green. She took a step, and her feet crunched down on the deep reddish brown wood chips that lined the path.

Adriana.

An aversion like nothing she'd ever known gripped her, and she struggled to keep her feet firmly planted, to not go forward into those woods. But an equally strong compulsion told her she had to. Something had happened here. Something important. The details danced just on the edge of her consciousness, teasing her, but not allowing her to reach them and remember.

A chill wind blew across her skin, starting as a breeze and growing stronger, and stronger. It picked up her hair, causing it to blow into her face and dance wildly around her head. The pale gown she was wearing plastered itself to her body, whipping around her calves. She held up an arm and squinted as leaves and bits of flying debris pelted her skin. Everything around her, everything inside her told her not to go forward, and yet she knew there was no choice. The leaves crackled and rustled around her feet, as if pushing her on. Ahead of her, the younger trees swayed back and forth, creaking mightily as the wind pushed them to their breaking point. They whipped back and forth, faster and faster. Her hair danced across her face. The leaves swirled around her, until the whole world started to turn brownish gray, and then…

…it all stopped.

She felt something in her hand, and looked down.

James's glasses. Tenderly, she brought the tortoiseshell frames closer to her face, remembering the laughing young man who'd worn them. But instead of having the spiderweb crack in the right lens, they were whole again.

Adriana.

Someone was calling her, and she couldn't see them, couldn't see anything but the trees right before her. But, oh, God, she knew that voice.

She gripped the glasses tightly. "Where are you?"

A low fog rolled across her path, suddenly rising up in thick gray tendrils, swirling into the trees. It wrapped around the trunks, until all she could see around her was a gray mist. She reached out, trying to get her bearings. The whole world seemed to tilt and swirl along with the fog.

And then, as suddenly as it had come, the mist started to settle. She could just make out the dark gray outlines of the trees again.

A figure appeared in a break in the woods. One she'd known well, once upon a time. Before her memories had started to fail her.

"James," she whispered, his name a prayer on her lips.

It had been so long since she'd seen him,

she'd forgotten his face, forgotten the sound of his voice, and she'd hated herself for forgetting. But even through the veil between them, she could sense what he looked like. She could remember.

The way his brown hair refused to lie flat no matter how many hair products he tried. The way he'd squint at her in the morning, half-blind and trying to make out her face without his glasses. How small children glommed on to his long legs as though he was their collective, long-lost best friend. How not-so-secretly charmed he was by them all.

The way he'd smiled shyly at her whenever she'd woken up before he had. The way he absolutely couldn't hold still, ever. Some part of him was always moving, even if it was just a toe, tapping in his sleep. The way he nearly fell over himself the first time he asked her out. The way he refused to go to sleep, after they'd been together for a while, without telling her he loved her.

It all came flooding back, and with it, an almost overwhelming sense of how grateful she was for every minute they'd had. He'd taught her so much, about living a life in service to others. About how to care for perfect strangers, even if they were dirty or coarse or even cruel. He'd cherished her, every minute they'd been together. And she'd cherished him right back.

"I miss you," she whispered, wondering if he could hear her, knowing he could.

She so much wanted him to say something to her; they'd been apart for so long. But for some reason, she seemed to take it as a given that he couldn't, so she just greedily drank in every minute they had, staring at each other through the veil between them, knowing that there was no way this could last. But, oh, she wished it could.

He lifted a hand, the way he used to wave goodbye whenever he walked her to her car in the morning.

"Don't go!" she cried. But if he heard her, he didn't give any indication. He turned around and walked back through the trees, disappearing over a small rise in the distance. The mist swirled back into place as if he'd never been there.

She knew she could have followed him, but somehow it didn't feel right. She had to go back. She'd see James again, but right now, she had to go back. There was something important she had to do.

Daniel.

She needed to see Daniel.

With one last look over her shoulder, she walked back down the oak- and cypress-lined path, until she arrived at a small clearing. Several decaying oaks had long ago fallen by the side and an enormous cypress towered over the path.

An unnatural silence descended on the forest. She started to pass under the cypress, and a swarm of black butterflies darted out from its low-hanging branches. They swooped and darted around her, and she turned to watch them disappear into the trees behind her.

When she turned back, a man stood directly in her path. Wearing a grotesque mask like the one she'd seen in her window.

"Adriana," the man whispered, his voice deeper, and unfamiliar. "Choose."

He pivoted to one side, sweeping his hand back like a macabre game-show host. Behind him, a figure lay on the ground, his face as still as death and one she knew well.

Daniel.

She felt James's glasses vanish from her grip. She looked down at her hands, only to find them covered with blood.

When she looked up again, the man in

the mask had stabbed a gleaming, serrated knife into the trunk of the cypress, just beside her head.

"Choose one, Adriana. Go ahead and choose."

She pushed past him and ran for all she was worth, knowing that when she got to Daniel, it still might be too late.

Behind her a killer's voice rang out.

"But I can still kill them both."

ADRIANA JACKKNIFED up in bed, willing herself awake, as her pulse thundered in her ears. Opening her eyes didn't do anything to help ease her fears—her bed didn't face this direction, her windows had curtains not blinds. Where…?

And then she saw Daniel, his body filling up the doorway, his skin tinged blue by the moonlight coming through the window. Gun in hand, he wore only a pair of sweatpants that hung low on his hips, and every muscle seemed tensed for a fight as he swept through the room.

She was nearly blindsided by relief at the sight of him. "Dream," she reassured him. "Just a dream."

The wild-eyed look left his face, and he calmly unloaded the clip from his semiautomatic, followed by a click as he ejected the chambered round, as well. He set the gun down on a nearby dresser, and then the mattress dipped as he sat down beside her.

"You okay, beautiful?" he asked, pushing a lock of hair off her forehead. He barely touched her skin, but somehow, that made her all the more aware of how close he was sitting. All she had to do was move…

"I'm sorry I woke you," she said. "I thought you were— I dreamt that he—" She couldn't even say the words, but fortunately, she didn't have to.

Cupping her face with one hand, he tilted his forehead until it touched hers, making their conversation that much more intimate and letting her know that this was reality. "I'm right here."

He was so close. She watched the rise and fall of his muscular chest, and suddenly she wanted to touch him, to feel all of that smooth, golden skin under her hands. She turned her head, pressed a kiss against his palm. "Thank you." The dream was already starting to loosen its hold. She could barely remember exactly what had made it so awful, except that something had threatened Daniel. And she knew how precious life was.

She dipped her head, skimmed her lips along his strong jawline, causing him to inhale sharply. He kept his body perfectly still, and she knew he was letting her make the decision. It wasn't a difficult one.

Her lips brushed his—an invitation, if he chose to take it that way. And, oh, how she wanted him to take it that way.

But instead, he pushed himself off the bed, raising his arms to shove his hair back as he stood.

"Don't go," she whispered.

"Think about what you want, Adriana."

She heard the springs of the mattress give as she rose, unable to think, because all she could do was feel. But somehow she knew instinctively that the way to handle his refusal was to show him everything she felt, once and for all.

She moved up behind him, pressing her body, covered only by a oversize T-shirt, against his bare back, feeling his muscles tense under her hands. Wrapping her arm around his waist, she ran her palm up his body, loving the feel of his smooth, bare skin, of the corrugated muscles of his abdomen, the light sprinkling of hair on his upper chest.

"I know what I want," she whispered, moving her lips against his spine.

He spun around, caught her wrist and just held it there, away from him, his chest heaving. He didn't say a word, but there was a definite challenge in his eyes.

And she knew exactly what he needed before he'd finish what they'd started.

She looked down at where his hand had coiled around her wrist. He loosened his grip but didn't let go.

Tenderly cupping the side of his face, she felt the rough whiskers of his five-o'clock shadow under her palm. "I haven't been able to feel much of anything in years. I haven't allowed myself to feel."

His face was impassive, his body so still he looked as if he were made of stone. The pale light filtering through the blinds dappled his skin, giving him an otherworldly look. She was getting to know that look well.

"But suddenly, when I'm with you, I feel everything," she said. "It scared me."

He closed his eyes, bowing his head into her touch. "I know the feeling," he murmured. And then he was looking right at her once more. "Are you sure, *mi amor?*"

"You're not second best, Daniel." She

meant those words more than she'd ever meant anything in her life. "I choose not to be afraid anymore. I choose you."

He smiled at her then—not the usual, reluctant half smile, but the sweetest, most unguarded smile she'd ever seen on his beautiful face. It took her breath away. Then his eyelids grew heavy and he bit his bottom lip, turning that smile into something more than a little wicked.

"Then come here, beautiful girl."

She didn't know who closed the space between them, but suddenly his mouth came down on hers. His kiss was sweet at first, but it quickly grew into something deeper, harder, more relentless. He spun her around so he had her up against the wall, running his hands up her arms until they were pinned lightly over her head, as he kissed and nibbled and sucked the skin of her neck, over her collarbone, down her chest.

She felt him inhale deeply as he tasted her, and she hooked one leg around his, wanting to be closer, wanting him so much. Letting go of her arms, he ran his hand up her thigh, shoving the cotton fabric of her T-shirt higher up her hips as he moved back up to capture her mouth with his.

She tangled her hands in his hair and kissed his face, his eyes, his neck, driving them both into a frenzied craziness she hadn't felt in way too long. Had she ever felt like this?

He tugged insistently at her shirt, so she stepped out of his arms and pulled the fabric over her head. He took a deep, shuddering breath as she dropped the shirt to the ground. Hooking her thumb under the waistband of her panties, she let them fall to the floor, as well. Slowly, almost reverently, he reached out and cupped the sides of her breasts, his fingers lightly teasing her nipples. Her legs suddenly weak, she fell back against the wall, letting it support her as he bent low to put his warm, wet mouth where his hands had been.

When she thought she couldn't stand it anymore, he felt so good, he rose and took her in his arms, and the shock of skin on skin made her gasp with pure pleasure.

"Beautiful girl," he breathed against her lips, and then his tongue plunged inside her mouth.

"Daniel," she gasped. "I want you. Right now."

A tender, private smile curving across his sensual mouth, he picked her up effortlessly in his arms and carried her to the bed. Laying her gently across the mattress, he braced himself above her with his arms, and she reached up to tug off his sweats. He clamped a hand gently across her wrist, though this time, both his face and his body told her he wanted her as much as she wanted him.

"Adriana, are you sure?"

She tugged at his arm, pulling him down to her, and trailed her fingers along his jawline. "More than anything in my life," she replied.

He leaned over and kissed her softly, his body trembling from the effort it took for him to hold back. "What about James?"

James.

She knew how much it had cost him to bring up that name right here, right now, and it was at that moment that she fell deeply and irrevocably in love with Daniel Cardenas.

She reached out and stroked the side of his face, tears welling up in her eyes. "James is gone," she said simply. "He loved me, and he would want me to be happy. And you, Daniel, *mi amor,* make me very happy."

He blinked at her, opening his mouth to respond. But when no words came out, he just crushed her mouth beneath his in a kiss that mingled both relief and desire, taking her breath away.

Addy wrapped her arms around Daniel and

held him tight, then pushed at his shoulders until he fell back on the bed. She helped him get rid of the last of his clothing, then swung one leg over his hips, straddling him. This was her decision, one she was committing to with all her heart, and she wanted him to know it—to know that everything they did and everything they felt was no accident, nothing she'd just fallen into. It was one hundred percent real, one hundred percent her choice. And his.

He skimmed his amazing hands across her skin, touching her in places that made her crazy as she made love to him. And then he was all she could see, all she could feel. Everything else was forgotten.

THE SUN HADN'T YET come up when Daniel felt Adriana move, her incredible body brushing against his before she left the bed they shared. He opened his eyes, already missing her and wanting to tell her so. But by then, she was already gone.

He could hear her soft footfalls padding down the hallway, and he waited, figuring she'd come back. But when the minutes ticked by and she didn't return, he got up, pulling on his pants to go look for her.

Following the yellow glow coming from the front of the house, he made his way through the living room and toward the kitchen. As he reached the doorway, the sound of Adriana's voice stopped him in his tracks.

She was sitting at the small breakfast table near the glass doors that opened up to a deck overlooking the park across the street. Instead of the cup of tea he expected her to have in her hand, she held a photograph. He didn't have to be a rocket scientist to figure out who was in that picture.

"Happy birthday, sweetheart," he heard her murmur, and then she kissed her fingertips and brushed them along the photo's surface.

The whole scene hit him like a punch to the gut. He knew it wasn't rational, knew she had every right to celebrate the birthday of someone who'd been so important to her. But he still had to wonder.

Was she having second thoughts? Could she have second thoughts after the night of knock-down, drag-out passion that they'd shared?

Would she stay with him when this was all over? Or would he have to send her back to her insulated, gray little world without risks, without him?

What if he lost her?

He was saved from contemplating that bleak scenario by a knock on the door. The sky was just beginning to lighten—he figured it was about 6:00 a.m., which was still too damn early to be getting visitors. So he went back to the bedroom and grabbed his gun before answering the door.

He needn't have bothered—it was just Borkowski. He unlocked the door, and as soon as he'd pulled it open, a blast of cold air hit him full in the face. She pushed past him and came inside, so he could close it again quickly. Apparently, the first fall frost had arrived.

"Get dressed," she ordered, pulling off her gloves and blowing on her hands. "I've got news."

"What happened, Liz?" Still wearing her T-shirt and little else, Adriana padded into the room. She pulled a red fleece blanket off the couch and wrapped it around her shoulders.

Borkowski looked her up and down and then took in Daniel's shirtless appearance. With a tart smirk, she sat down on the couch. "Well, your friend Jason woke up, for one."

He felt a pang of guilt at not going to see his friend while he'd been laid up in the hospital. He'd called every day, though, only to be told that the staff was still keeping Jason sedated while his abdominal wound and collapsed lung healed. "How is he?"

"Doing well. But here's the kicker. He ID'd one Sean Cantrell." She turned to Addy. "You know, the skateboarder you attacked the other day? ID'd him as a guy he said was lurking around Addy's house along with the masked man, when he was attacked. We've got a pretty solid connection between Jason and Addy's attacker and that grubby little high schooler."

Especially since said grubby little high schooler had shown up here the other day with a knife and an MO similar to whoever had left the threats at Addy's door. "Need me to come down and talk to him?"

Borkowski shook her head. "No, been there, done that. We told his parents what kind of charges he'd be facing, and they came down on him. He sang like a canary." Reaching into her coat pocket, she pulled out a slim, plastic case that contained a computer CD. "It's all part of some game that's being distributed underground, among teenage technogeeks, for the most part."

He took the case from her, prying it open to reveal a blue CD-RW with a single word scrawled across the top in black marker. "Mortifera," he read.

"Deadly things," Adriana immediately replied. He narrowed his eyes at her, but he didn't need to ask the question on his mind. "It's Latin. Means *deadly things*."

"You know Latin?"

She tapped her temple. "Head full of game-show trivia, remember?"

"Somehow I doubt that would be on a game show," he replied, impressed.

"Basically the kid says that a lot of what's been happening to you over the years—the notes, the knives in your door, prank phone calls—are part of the game. You get to a certain level, and then you need to do something in real time and submit proof to get instructions from the game master on how to download the next level." Borkowski rolled her eyes. "Apparently, the kids in your neighborhood thought you were the game master. That's why Cantrell didn't run when you confronted him."

A small, thin line appeared between her eyebrows as Adriana wrinkled her nose in disbelief. "The game master? Seriously?"

"Seriously. You are in a world of cool according to Cantrell. One of the rules was they were never to talk to you, or you'd have probably had a little fan club at your doorstep." She gestured with her chin toward the disk Daniel held. "I thought you might want to look at it, since you used to investigate computer crimes. See if you can get anything off it. The game is basically torture porn—with puzzles," she said. "The women's faces are always hidden, but…Daniel, some of it looks too real. And that Web site you found with Addy's photos on it? Guess who posted it?"

"The game master," Daniel supplied.

"Right. One of the real-time tasks of the game was to take a picture of Addy without her seeing you and manipulate it into something gross to post on the site. Whoever really is the game master is quite obsessed with Adriana. And violence against women in general."

"Why in the world would a bunch of teenagers think I'd create a game about my own really nasty murder?" Adriana asked, pulling the blanket tighter around her body.

"Yeah, kind of far-fetched, isn't it?" Liz reached up to brush at something in the corner of her eye. "It's not completely impossible, though. Look at the horror films that are out now—torture porn is in."

"They must've thought I was letting my freak flag fly sky-high, if I'd do that."

Adriana made a noise that could have been a laugh—a really angry one. "No wonder they always looked at me so strangely whenever I met them outside. I probably scared them on some level."

"So, here's the big news…" Liz began.

"Oh, God, there's more?" Adriana covered her face with her hands for a second, then pulled them back to cup her cheeks.

Liz held up a hand. "No, this is good." Reaching up, she unbuttoned her coat, extracting a manila folder she'd kept tucked inside until now. "We got the report back on the Sanchez murder from the medical examiner. Turns out, Janie Sanchez was sexually assaulted. Perp used a condom, but it leaked."

Daniel took the folder she held out, flipping it open. "Get a hit on CODIS?" he asked. CODIS, or the combined DNA Index System, was an FBI-run database of DNA profiles submitted by local, state and federal agencies. If Janie's killer had ever had a major run-in with the law, his DNA would likely be in CODIS.

"Sure did. Stan Peterson."

Holy— "Got him in custody?"

"Last night," Borkowski confirmed. "Got

a warrant for his computer, too, and the Electronic Crimes Department found all sorts of good stuff on it, including some interesting poetry about Adriana. They're still sorting through data, but all signs point to Peterson being the Mortifera game master."

"What about that photo of James? The one with his glasses? And the glasses themselves?" Addy asked.

"We're looking into it," said Liz. "Right now, we can't explain it. We've established that Stan wasn't living in California when Carter was active in our area, so he couldn't have taken that photo. Could be doctored. Our people should be able to confirm this in the next few days."

Daniel couldn't help but feel a sense of letdown. Of course, his primary feeling was one of relief—that they'd nailed Peterson, that Adriana was safe and no more women would have to die the way Janie Sanchez had. But it all seemed anticlimactic somehow—he'd always assumed that when they caught the guy who'd killed Janie and had terrorized Adriana, he himself would be right in the middle of it all. Not sitting around on the sidelines, twiddling his thumbs.

Okay, so he hadn't been twiddling his

thumbs. Instead, he'd spent the best night of his life with the most amazing woman he'd ever met. Who might or might not still be too wrapped up in mourning her dead fiancé to love him back.

Love. He flipped the CD back and forth in his hand, causing the plastic case to rattle. That word should have scared the hell out of him. It should have felt like too much, too soon.

But instead it just…was.

He stole a glance at Adriana, who sat lost in thought. Liz cleared her throat and smacked her palms on her thighs as she stood.

"Well, I'd better get going," she said, shooting Daniel a knowing look. "I'm sure you two have a lot to talk about." She headed for the door, stopping just as she reached it, her hand on the knob. "And you have two days remaining of your vacation, by the way," she said over her shoulder as she left, the door clicking closed behind her.

Adriana rose and walked over to him, her dark hair tousled and her skin clear and soft and free of any makeup. She looked so beautiful he wanted to grab hold of her and beg her to stay. But of course, he didn't.

"I can go home?"

He nodded. "Sure."

"Wow." She blew her long, diagonal bangs off her forehead as she contemplated that news. "It's really over." And then she leaned over and planted the softest kiss on his cheek. He closed his eyes, and when he opened them again, she had straightened once more and was no longer touching him. "Thank you. For everything."

"Anytime."

Her amber eyes flicked down to stare at the floor. "Daniel, about last night—"

His jaw clenched so hard he almost felt his teeth crack. Hell, he really didn't want to hear whatever it was that was coming next. Not that. Not after everything.

"I meant everything I said to you." She reached for him then, wrapping her arms around his neck, and the relief he felt almost undid him. "But I just need a couple of days. Just to get my head on straight. Get used to the idea of not being the same person I was...before."

Her fingers caressed the back of his neck, toying with the short hair at his nape and sending chills across his body. He leaned forward and planted a soft kiss on her forehead to let her know he understood.

She bit her lower lip, as if unsure of what his response would be. "Wait for me?"

"Always," he replied.

The smile she gave him then would have lasted him a hundred years—but he was damned glad she wasn't asking him to wait that long. He pulled her back into his arms, losing himself in the feel of her, in the scent of her hair and the warmth of her skin.

"You know, I wasn't sure what you were going to say," she murmured against his throat. "You're not exactly the easiest guy in the world to read."

"Then read this." He pulled back and looked her straight in the eye. "Last night was the best night of my life. Before you go, I wanted you to know it."

Chapter Twelve

With the memory of Daniel's kiss on her lips, Adriana went back to her house. Though she missed him, it was good to be home. Because before she could move on, she actually, physically, had to move on.

Grabbing a cardboard box out of her garage, she brought it into her living room and set it down in the middle of the coffee table. She walked over to the matching sofa table on the far wall, covered up by a black runner on which several framed photos of her and James rested. She picked up the picture in the center. It had always been one of her favorites.

A friend had taken it of the two of them right outside her home, on the beach. James was laughing, his head thrown back and his glasses slightly askew. His brown hair was as tousled and unmanageable as ever, and a white dot of ice cream dripped off the end of his nose. She was by his side, a wide grin on her face, holding the incriminatory vanilla cone. Her hair was short, with caramel-brown highlights and a few random cherry-red streaks in it just for fun. She wore a flowy, empire-waisted red dress with a turquoise pattern that, amazingly, worked instead of being garish. A giant pair of turquoise-and-silver earrings dangled from her ears. She remembered when she'd loved to dress up for him. She remembered what it felt like not to be afraid.

She remembered Daniel. Because of him, she remembered love.

That photo would remain in a place of honor. But the rest…she collected them all and gently stacked them inside the box. Someday she'd take them out of their frames and put them in an album, so she'd always have them. But for now, the box would do.

Pulling the black runner off the table, she wadded it up into a ball and tossed it into the box, too. She'd tied her red scarf around her hair again when she'd dressed at Daniel's. Unfastening it from her hair, she laid it on the table, smoothing it out. And then she put the one picture she'd saved of herself with James on top of it.

She spent the entire weekend cleaning her whole house, taking down pale curtains and replacing them with the vibrant sari silks and brilliantly colored cotton voile panels she'd kept stored in her attic. Pictures went into the box, along with dull throw pillows and nearly her entire candle collection. She got her old art pieces down from the attic, and once they were in their old places on her walls and shelves, her home looked like… her home again.

Tossing a fuzzy, brilliant aqua throw over the couch, she headed to her master suite and tackled her wardrobe next, stuffing nearly everything black she owned into bags for Goodwill, except for a few staples like the little black dress. If she never wore another black piece of clothing in her life, she figured she could probably live with herself.

Throwing open her windows, she let the cool, fall breeze come in, not caring that the weather was getting colder and that she almost needed a jacket.

The chime of the doorbell interrupted her appreciation of fresh air. She knew Daniel wouldn't come over—he'd promised he'd give her a few days, and she knew he wouldn't go back on that. But she couldn't help but hope.

When she looked through the peephole, however, she saw a dark blue-uniformed Monterey cop standing on her front stoop, wearing a pair of mirrored sunglasses similar to Daniel's.

Daniel.

There was only one reason a Monterey cop who wasn't Liz or Daniel would come to her door.

Oh, God.

Scrabbling for the dead bolt, she slammed it back, unlocking the door and flinging it open. "What's happened?" she demanded of the cop. "Did something happen to Daniel?"

"No, ma'am. Daniel's fine." The man appeared to be in his midthirties, with a military haircut and a solid fireplug of a body. His shirt buttons strained to cover his stocky chest, which seemed odd, given what she knew about the department dress regulations. "May I come in?"

She stepped back to let him enter. "Sure. What can I help you with?"

As soon as he'd shut the door, he removed his sunglasses, folding them up and neatly tucking them into his breast pocket. And then he reached up again, picking at the skin on his right cheekbone to loosen it. He peeled the skin, until a prosthetic piece lifted off the entire upper portion of his face, revealing a network of vicious-looking scars.

His face split into an eerie smile, and she started to back away from him. Despite the scars, she knew that face. She'd seen it on countless newspapers and on TV. She'd seen it in her nightmares for four years.

"Hello, Adriana," he said.

With a loud grunt the man she knew as Elijah Carter leaped forward, swinging something large and heavy at her temple. And then everything went black.

THE TWO DAYS since he'd last seen Adriana dragged by, making Daniel realize that he'd never had a more miserable vacation in his life. Figuring he might as well make himself useful, he hauled his laptop out to the kitchen table and fired it up, inserting the Mortifera disk into the CD player.

From what he'd been able to gather, talking to Borkowski and Lockwood, Peterson hadn't yet cracked, still maintaining his innocence—in a loud and whiny way, no doubt. The guy kept insisting that "the scarred man" was the game master and had put him up to everything. Of course, when it came to providing any details about said "scarred man," other than that he was, well, scarred, Stan came up seriously short. And he would only admit to stalking Adriana in the name of the game.

When they'd confronted him about his DNA being found at the Sanchez crime scene, he'd broken down and told them the scarred man had exploited his weakness. He'd never meant for Janie to die.

Right.

The D.A. had sent in one of the county shrinks to evaluate Stan before trial. Lockwood had suggested to Daniel that perhaps the psychiatrist should be sure to evaluate both of Peterson's personalities.

Something still felt off about it all, though. Which was why he was spending the weekend playing Peterson's twisted game, instead of heading out to Addy's and doing his best to charm her into smiling at him again.

The CD whirred in the drive, and then the screen went blank. A few seconds ticked by, and a woman's body flickered into view. The creator of the game had set up the video to simulate an old movie reel—complete with flickering images and dust particles floating across the screen. The woman wore a filthy shift, and she'd been blindfolded and gagged with equally filthy rags. She knelt on the floor, her head bent over her knees so her matted hair fell into her face. Someone had tied a hangman's noose around her neck, which hung slack, for the moment.

One by one, nine dashes appeared on the screen.

Hangman. The first puzzle was Hangman.

Sean Cantrell had been a big help, providing the answers to the levels he'd passed. Unfortunately, the puzzles never appeared in the same order for any player, so Daniel was left with nearly fifty answers to sort through. He figured it'd be faster to just play.

"*D*." He pressed the key on his laptop keyboard.

The noose tightened, not enough to strangle the woman completely, but enough that she had to raise up on her knees. The accompanying sound effects—of a woman choking and gagging—seemed all too real. He hated to think of how Peterson had recorded them.

"Okay, no *D*," he muttered to the screen. "*M*."

An *M* slowly appeared in the first blank, followed by the sound of a female sob.

Too easy. He typed in *M-O-R-T-I-F-E-R-A*. A shrill scream pierced the air, and then a skull appeared on the screen, laughing maniacally.

"Nice one. I think I saw that graphic on YouTube." He scowled at it, punching the return button.

As the afternoon wore on, he played through the rest of the puzzles, each one more disturbing than the last. For some reason, whenever the game hooked him up to the Web—the point where Sean had said players received instructions for real-world tasks to perform—the site just spat the next pass code at him so he could keep playing on his computer.

Maybe Peterson had disabled the real-world function so he wouldn't incriminate himself. Whatever the case, without that extra hassle, Daniel got through most of the game quickly. When he reached the final level, the cursor turned into a knife, and the photo of Adriana's face superimposed on another woman's naked and bleeding body flashed into view.

With a curse, Daniel waited for his last instructions.

They appeared letter by letter, white

against the black screen, as if someone were typing them.

I'll steal her voice, I'll pluck her soul out.

His hands clenched into fists, Daniel felt a rage so pure go through him, he knew he would have killed Stan Peterson if he'd been in the same room. Reluctantly, he dragged the knife cursor over the woman's throat, underneath Adriana's face.

The next directive slowly appeared on screen.

I'll slice her fingers, one by one.

Swallowing hard, he clicked the knife cursor on each of the woman's hands, once for each finger.

This time, the words flashed as one.

She begs to die, but I won't let her. Not until I say it's done.

Another damned verse. In that telltale iambic rhythm.

Seventeen blanks appeared on the screen, as they had in the Hangman puzzle, arranged in three groups. And then a woman's voice, saying something that sounded like gibberish.

"Sssssssivell. Errrrr-ehtrrrack. Haj-eeyahlee."

What the hell?

"Sssssssivell. Errrrr-ehtrrrack. Haj-eeyah-lee."

He clicked all over the screen, but he couldn't get the voice to stop without turning down the volume or shutting the computer down completely. But by what sounded like the four-hundredth repetition, it occurred to him that what he'd thought was gibberish sounded an awful lot like the noises his grandmother's old turntable had made when he'd played her record albums backward as a kid.

Minimizing the game screen, he fired up a sound-editing program he had and set it to record. It did so, displaying the woman's message in a visual sound-wave pattern. With a few taps of his keyboard, he asked the program to play the message backward.

"Elijah Carter lives."

He'd know that voice in his sleep. Addy's voice. Oh, God.

The woman's body faded, and the skull with its flapping lower jaw flew across the screen, its shrieking laughter piercing the air. The last verse of the poem flashed at the bottom of the screen.

Steal her voice, I'll pluck her soul out.
Slice her fingers, one by one.

She begs to die, but I won't let her.
Not until I say it's done.

Knocking over his chair in his haste to get to a phone, Daniel grabbed the receiver and punched in Adriana's number.

It rang and rang, until finally the machine picked up. "Addy, it's Daniel. This is urgent. If you're there, pick up."

Please, please pick up.

Several precious seconds ticked by. "You must call me, as soon as you get this. It's urgent." He hung up and dialed her cell phone, leaving the same message when the call went to voice mail.

The next call he made was to Liz.

"Borkowski," she snapped.

"Liz, I need you to send a patrol car to Adriana's house, right now. Have them verify whether she's there or not."

"Cardenas, what's wrong?" He could hear her directing someone at the station to dispatch the blue-and-white, which provided some measure of relief.

"If she's not there… I can't believe we missed it, Liz. Stan might be right—Elijah Carter might still be alive, and if he is, he's got Adriana."

WHEN ADRIANA OPENED her eyes, a thin film seemed to have settled over them, blurring her vision and giving everything she could see a kind of halo. Her limbs felt heavy and her head thick and ponderous. She wondered why her bed was so uncomfortable, why her hands were pinned above her head.

A face swam into view.

With a gasp she shrank back, and everything became suddenly clear.

She was alone. In a deserted house somewhere remote. With Elijah Carter.

She heard the sing of metal on leather, and then he waved the blade of a large, serrated hunting knife in front of her face.

She bit down on her tongue to keep from screaming.

He caressed her cheek with the flat surface of the blade, the metal cool against her skin. Her wrists burned from the fishing line he'd used to tie her to the small cot on which she lay. His eyes burned with a horrible mixture of lust and insanity.

He didn't say a word to her, and she knew he wouldn't. He was waiting for her to say something, waiting for her to scream. She didn't want to give him that satisfaction. He fed off fear, and there was no appealing to his humanity, because there wasn't any inside him.

He dragged the tip of the knife across her chin, down her neck. She was shaking uncontrollably now, and she tried to tilt her chin upward and away from the sharp edge, but he followed her movements. The tip scratched her as it made its way down the fragile skin of her throat, between her breasts, down to her stomach.

He let it hover there, over her abdomen.

She knew what he liked to do to women's stomachs. She knew what he liked to do with knives.

Suddenly his lips pulled back in a horrible grimace, and he drew the blade hard across her skin.

Oh, God, it hurt. It hurt so much. She bucked her body against the pain, thrashing against the bonds that pinned her wrists and ankles, but the pain wouldn't stop. And then she was screaming, so loud and so long, she was sure someone had to hear her. But no one came.

He just laughed. And then he wrapped his big hands around her throat, squeezing until she couldn't scream anymore.

Chapter Thirteen

Daniel burst into the police station, striding through the main office with one hell-bent purpose driving him forward.

"Where's Peterson?" he growled as Liz fell into step beside him.

"Interrogation room four, waiting for you."

The patrol car hadn't found Adriana at home. Worse, the front door had been wide-open, and the living room looked as if a tornado had hit: broken glass, overturned furniture and books were everywhere. Someone had definitely broken into her home. And Adriana had fought him like a wild woman.

Please, God, don't let me be too late.

He stormed into the interrogation room, the door slamming against the wall as he entered. "Where is she?"

Peterson regarded him dully. "Where is who?"

"Adriana Torres." He leaned across the table and got right in Peterson's face.

"How should I know?" he answered calmly.

"Who is the scarred man?" Daniel shouted.

"I don't know."

"Is he Elijah Carter?"

Stan's sleepy eyes widened, and he rose up from his habitual slouch. "I don't…I don't know."

"It wasn't you at Adriana's house that night, it was Carter, right? You couldn't have dragged Jason halfway down the beach." He rained questions at Peterson like bullets.

"I don't know what you're talking about."

"You told us last time you knew about Carter's past murders, including that of James Brentwood," Liz interjected. "You know who Carter is, Stan."

Stan started to cry, sloppy, heaving sobs that didn't make Daniel feel the least bit sorry for him.

"Who is the scarred man?" Daniel asked again.

"I can't tell you." Peterson rubbed his eyes with his grubby sleeve.

"Where is he now?"

"I can't tell you!" he shouted, dissolving

into ugly sobs once more, his face red and growing puffier every second.

"Why can't you tell us, Stan?" Leaning across the table, Liz placed one hand over his, keeping her voice gentle, nurturing.

"He'll hurt me. He'll kill me."

"Stan, have you heard of Pelican Bay?" Daniel asked in a low voice. When the man didn't respond, Daniel moved in closer, speaking right in his ear. "It's a level-four, maximum-security prison for some of the most violent offenders in the state of California. And I will personally make sure you end up there if Adriana dies, do you hear me?" He slammed a hand on the table, causing Stan to jump in his chair. "The inmates up there don't take too kindly to serial killers—or their accomplices. They hate them almost as much as they hate pedophiles and child killers."

All of a sudden Stan stopped crying. Wiping his nose on his sleeve, he straightened, took a deep breath and composed himself. Staring at Daniel with his watery blue eyes, he looked like a completely different person from the one who'd been sniveling a few seconds earlier.

"That whore deserves whatever she gets," he snarled.

Daniel didn't think, he just acted. He slammed his fist into Peterson's face, the blow reverberating up his entire arm.

"Cardenas, what the hell?" With a metallic screech, Borkowski shoved her chair back and leaped to her feet.

For the first time in his life, he'd abused his position as a defender of the law. And he didn't give a damn. As Peterson hunched over in his chair, moaning softly and cradling his face, Borkowski practically shoved Daniel out the door, her eyes snapping blue fire.

"You will not *ever* lay your hand on a prisoner again, I don't care if he's holding your entire extended family and the President of the United States hostage!" she shouted, jabbing him in the shoulder. "I am putting you on report for excessive force used against a person in our custody."

Precious seconds ticked by as they glared at each other, breathing hard.

"And I'll do it tomorrow," she continued. She grabbed him by both shoulders. "Daniel, you know you can get this information out of him. Get in there and do it before we lose her." And then she practically shoved him back in the room.

When Adriana awoke again, her throat felt so raw and swollen she couldn't understand how she could still breathe. Instinctively, she jerked against the bonds that held her, but they just cut into her skin even more.

Opening her eyes as little as possible, hoping she'd still appear unconscious if Carter was still in the room, she scanned her surroundings.

She seemed to be in a workroom of some sort. No drywall covered the beams in the walls. The far wall had a workbench along it. And she could hear footsteps downstairs, which meant she was alone, for now.

But he'd come back. He always came back.

And from what she knew about Carter's killing methods, it was only going to get worse. She couldn't hear any sounds other than those that Carter or she herself made, so she'd long ago guessed they were in a remote area.

Daniel and Liz thought they had Janie Sanchez's murderer in custody. And she'd told Daniel to leave her alone. No one was coming for her. No one would know she was missing for days.

A hoarse sob escaped her swollen throat. Oh, God, she didn't want to die like this. She didn't know if she could stand any more pain, or the anticipation of what was going to come.

Could she will herself to die, just so this could all be over? She closed her eyes, wondered if she should sleep. Maybe she'd be lucky and she wouldn't wake up.

Some remote part of her brain that wasn't operating on a primal, animal level conjured up Daniel's face. The way he looked at her the last time she'd seen him, his hazel eyes as soft as his touch. He'd blame himself. So would Liz.

Looking to her right, she saw a thick, rusted wire poking through the fabric of the box spring on which she lay, close enough, that if she just bent her hand, like this… With only the tiniest range of motion, she moved the fishing line that cut into her wrist across the edge of the wire. Back and forth, back and forth, as if it were the only thing that mattered in the world.

A floorboard creaked from another part of the house, and then footfalls clumped in her direction. She closed her eyes, pretending to be asleep. She heard him enter the room, tried not to let her eyelids flutter when he turned the light—a bare bulb swinging on a wire above them—on again.

And then he sat down beside her, putting

part of his weight on the box spring. She felt his hand on her hip, tried not to recoil when his hot, foul breath hit her face.

Closer. Closer still.

Her eyes flew open. Yanking her wrist free, she jabbed her thumb into his eye. With a howl, he jerked back, clutching his meaty hands over his eye.

Frantically, she scratched and pulled at the line immobilizing her other wrist, trying to free her other hand before…

Suddenly, unexpectedly, he stopped shouting, straightened his spine, his back still to her, and dropped his hands to his sides. Then he turned around, his black eyes shining like obsidian.

He pulled the evil knife free of its scabbard and held it up in front of his face. He was laughing.

Daniel, I'm sorry.

DANIEL SAT DOWN across from Peterson, placing a notepad and a pencil in the center of the table. No more intimidation. No more games. Peterson himself had told him his motive, and if this didn't work… This had to work. They were running out of time.

Clamping his hand over his watch, so he

wouldn't lose his composure because too much time was ticking away, he laid his hands on top of the table. "Stan, I worked on the task force that hunted Elijah Carter last time around." Gasping, he had to look away for a second. The image of Adriana, lying on a floor somewhere, bloody and raw the way he'd seen Janie Sanchez, blindsided him. It pressed against his chest, made him want to scream at the man in frustration. But shouting wasn't going to help Adriana anymore. Only his cop instincts had a prayer of doing that.

Reaching into a manila folder he'd brought in with him, Daniel extracted a photo of one of Carter's victims from four years ago—the one he'd taken the most time with. He placed it on the table and pushed it over toward Peterson. "This is what Carter does to women."

Peterson looked away.

"This is what he's doing to Adriana," Daniel continued.

Pressing his lips together into a tight, white line, Peterson began to rock back and forth in his chair.

"The DNA evidence shows you sexually assaulted Janie Sanchez just before she was murdered. You were part of the game, weren't you, Stan? You got higher than anyone before." He had to work to keep his voice politely encouraging, when what he really wanted to do was slam the man's head into the table until he spilled his guts. "You earned the right to come with Carter when he attacked Janie Sanchez. And you forced her to have sex with you."

Peterson flinched, and he still wouldn't look at Daniel. "But you thought it would end there, didn't you? You didn't know he was going to kill her, did you, Stan?" The words he uttered weren't ones he believed for a second, but that was how interrogation worked. You did what you could to absolve the subject of blame so he'd feel safe enough to confess. "And you couldn't have known it was going to take so long."

Swiping at his eyes, Peterson was visibly shaking now.

"You can stop that from happening to Adriana. She was sweet to you. Whatever you think of me, she was always sweet to you." He leaned forward, silently praying that this would work. "Help me, Stan. Be the hero. This is your chance to be the hero, be *her* hero." Finally Peterson turned his head to face Daniel, though he still couldn't quite meet Daniel's eye. "I swear, when I find

Elijah Carter, you won't have to worry about him ever again."

A long silence descended on the grim little room. And then Stan reached forward and pulled the notepad and pencil toward him. He scribbled down an address.

"I gave him the keys to my mother's cottage south of Carmel," Stan mumbled. "He would have taken her there."

Chapter Fourteen

The address Stan gave them was at least a half-hour drive from the police station, with lights on and sirens blaring. By the time Liz and Daniel found the house—in a wooded neighborhood set back a quarter mile from the road—he'd nearly gone mad from thinking about what Carter could do to Adriana in all that time.

He had to keep believing she was still alive, but that possibility was painful, too. If she was still alive, it was because Carter was making her suffer—and enjoying it.

Of course, Daniel would enjoy making Carter suffer, even more.

Slamming the car into Park halfway down the driveway, he hurled himself out and approached the house on foot, Liz following close behind. They'd called for full SWAT backup, but given that they'd barreled out of the parking lot seconds after Peterson gave up the address, the two of them were at least twenty minutes ahead of that backup.

And there was no way in hell either one of them was going to wait twenty minutes.

"Peterson said there are two stories and no basement," Liz said, as they circled the house, looking for the best way in. He nodded, and she said, "I've got your back. Go."

Guns drawn, they looked in all of the windows, but could see no signs of life inside. The house looked normal, from its delicate lace curtains to the cheery yellow paint in the kitchen. You'd never think a murderer lived there, even temporarily.

Once they'd tacitly agreed to head in through the back, Liz carefully peeled open the screen door, and Daniel reached for the knob, slowly turning it in the hopes that it would be unlocked.

It was.

Swiftly, silently, they entered the house, listening for any sounds of activity. They heard none.

The house spread out from the entrance—kitchen and dining room directly to their left, living room and family room beyond that, bedrooms flanking either side. Plenty of places to watch them in secret. Plenty of places to hide.

Daniel scanned the kitchen. A 1950s-style clock in the shape of a cat leered at him, its tail swishing silently as each second passed. A couple of birds darted across the window.

Two doors sat on either end of the small space. He motioned toward one, and Liz moved in closer to watch his back and sides while he did so. They silently crept across the square-patterned linoleum. Daniel put his hand on the doorknob and slowly, carefully turned it. He pulled the door open, his Smith & Wesson at the ready.

An enormous crash resounded through the house. Empty paint cans tumbled down onto the floor of the pantry, rolling at their feet.

"Well, he knows we're here now," Liz muttered.

No longer bothering to keep quiet, they just moved, heading into the dining room, the front hallway. The whole house was filled with giant pieces of furniture—huge ornate mirrors and heavy antique armoires. Gave the place more nooks and crannies than any home should be allowed to have—and slowed them down as they stopped to check around them all.

So far, the house was deathly silent—no sign of Carter or Adriana.

Shhhhhhh.

As they headed into the living room, the faintest sound, like cloth brushing against drywall, set Daniel on high alert. He swung his arm out to keep Borkowski from going any farther into the room, and stopped. Listened. His eyes were drawn to the dim staircase against the wall on their right, flanked by a heavy oak banister.

The living room enjoyed plenty of light from the enormous windows along the east and south walls, but all of that light dimmed noticeably the farther it got up the staircase. Daniel could practically hear Carter breathing, sitting quietly in the darkness at the top, like a spider waiting for its fly to come closer.

Careful to stay along the wall, Daniel crept forward, Borkowski coming up close behind. One step. Two. Three.

He heard a click, and then...a flash. Three gunshots, in rapid-fire succession. Coming from the top of the stairs.

Borkowski grunted, her head jerking forward, arms flailing, as one of them hit her square in the chest. She stumbled back, a look of disbelief on her face.

Daniel returned fire, bullets splintering the banister and sending wood shards flying in every direction. "Liz!" he shouted.

Then he saw her fall.

Footfalls pounded above them as Carter moved away from the stairs. Gun still pointing at the top of the staircase, Daniel sidestepped over to Borkowski, whose eyes were glazed and staring at the ceiling.

"Liz?" He put two fingers on her carotid pulse.

She smacked them away. With a sharp "eeeeeeee," she greedily sucked in a huge lungful of air, the bullet having knocked the wind out of her. Lurching upright into a sitting position, she erupted into a series of harsh coughs, her brown curls falling into her eyes as she hunched forward.

"Kevlar works," Daniel remarked dryly, still keeping an eye on the staircase as he shielded her with his body.

Still coughing, although a little less harshly, Borkowski pointed at her leg.

Her knee looked as if it had been shattered by a second bullet. When he looked at her face again, it was pale and drawn from the pain. "Can't walk," she choked.

With a curse, he yanked a scarf off a

nearby table and wadded it up, pressing it against Liz's knee to stanch the bleeding. Hissing at the pressure, she took it from him to hold it in place herself. He walked around her and grabbed her under the shoulders, dragging her as gently as he could to a corner in the room where she'd be out of the line of fire from the stairs.

"Daniel? You're not—"

But before she could finish her question, he was bounding up the stairs, two at a time. At the top was a dim hallway, with closed doors flanking each side of it.

Shoving the first door open so it slammed against the wall, he swept his gun throughout the room.

Clear. Unless Carter was hiding under the bed. The room had no closet—just a small armoire.

He did the same in the second room and the third.

The fourth was a large master bedroom, and it did have a closet door, which had been cracked open about an inch. His cop sense on full alert, he inched forward, leading with his Smith & Wesson.

When he reached the door, which opened toward him, he flattened himself against the wall on the hinge side. Stretching out an arm, he curled his fingers around the door's edge. One…two… He pulled it toward him, stepped out, took aim.

Instead of the small closet he'd expected, a whole room sat behind that door, the walls bare beams and plywood. A single naked lightbulb swung overhead, illuminating a woman's body lying on a rusted cot.

Adriana.

Something strong and painful squeezed his chest, until his ribs felt as if they'd been crushed. She was so still. Pale. Her wrists swollen and raw where they were bound to the cot frame, her ankles bloody. Two vicious cuts had been sliced across her stomach, and a band of bruises bloomed just above her collarbone. She was the mirror image of Carter's past victims, of the crime-scene photos that even now lay on his desk. He couldn't see her face, as it was turned away from him. He couldn't tell if she were still breathing.

Oh, God, please let her still be breathing.

When he reached her, he saw that a serrated-edge hunting knife lay by her side. Would Carter have left that near her if she were still alive?

"Adriana," he choked out, reaching out to touch her.

Cold. Her skin was cold.

And then, a sound behind him. A hiss of satisfaction.

He swung around. Fired a shot at the doorway as a shadow ducked back out of sight.

Advancing, Daniel fired off another shot. And another, taking a huge chunk out of the door frame.

"Carter!" he shouted, a fury unlike any he'd ever known fueling his every move.

When he reached the doorway, he scanned the room, then swung around to the left and fired several shots into the wall.

Carter was gone.

Impossible. Daniel had had the room's exit in his line of sight the entire time.

He heard another noise, the faintest exhalation. He looked up. Carter had flattened himself against a corner of the ceiling, his feet spread, one braced on the wall, one on the side of the armoire. He swung his gun hand up, aiming for Daniel's head.

Daniel threw his weight back, and he felt the bullet whiz past his chest as he dove into the room where Addy lay. Landing hard on his side, he scrambled to get up, to keep one of Carter's bullets from hitting Addy as a shadow fell into the room.

Daniel fired his gun at the doorway as a shot rang out.

Something slammed into his chest, and then his leg, sending a fiery pain throughout his body. His gun slipped from his fingers and slid across the floor. Carter advanced on him, a slow grin spreading across his pale face. The wind had been knocked out of him, and Daniel still couldn't get any air. Crawling backward, desperately trying to breathe, Daniel reached for his gun.

He heard a click. Carter pulled back the hammer on his single-action semiautomatic.

A thud behind him. Adriana's body had rolled off the cot. Carter looked up.

With a sharp inhale, Daniel felt the air return to his lungs as he simultaneously kicked out at Carter's knee. The man's body buckled.

Another shot rang out. Carter windmilled backward, his hands clutching his chest. His gun dropped to the floor with a clatter. Another shot hit him in the shoulder. Still another in the chest.

And then one final one in the center of his forehead, a red rosette blooming just underneath his hairline. The stocky man tottered, his mouth an *O* of disbelief. And then he fell.

Daniel turned around, vaulting to his feet.

Adriana stood there, pale and bloody, still aiming his gun at the space where Carter had stood.

"You will *not* kill them both," she slurred. And then her knees started to buckle.

Daniel caught her before she fell.

Chapter Fifteen

Though Daniel put up a huge fight at the hospital, the doctors wouldn't allow him to ignore the bullet wound in his leg while they treated Adriana. As soon as they'd bandaged him up, however, he was by her side, where he remained for three days. They didn't talk about what had happened. For the most part he just sat with her and watched her sleep.

Her wounds weren't serious, in the medical sense, but he had no idea what her mental state would be after the painkillers wore off and she had to face what had happened.

She'd been at the mercy of a killer for twelve hours—the man who'd killed her fiancé. She'd watched Daniel get shot by that man. And it'd be his face she would associate with the two worst days of her life, from this day forward.

But he'd associate her face with the best days of his.

He took her hand, listened to her breathe and watched and waited until she woke up again.

He must've fallen asleep, because the next thing he knew, someone was stroking his hair. He looked up to find Adriana smiling softly at him.

"About time you woke up," she said.

"Adriana," he breathed.

"Is he gone?"

He knew right away who she meant. "Carter?" He nodded, wondering if she even remembered shooting him. "Yes, he's definitely dead this time." He wanted to pull her into his arms, but he wondered if that's what she wanted. Instead he just took her hand, caressing her knuckles with his thumb.

"I just want you to know, I don't want to talk about what happened. You know what he does to women, and you saw what he did to me. It's over, and I don't want to relive it ever again. I don't want to give him any more power over me." That speech seemed to have exhausted her, and she fell back against her pillows with a sigh. "You saved me, didn't you?"

"I helped," he replied. "You saved yourself." The doctors had said it was a miracle she could stand, in her weakened condition, after losing all that blood. It was a miracle she could fire a gun—and that her aim had been true. Thank God she'd been so strong. Thank God she'd stayed alive, even if she walked away from all of this and left him behind, too.

"It was your face I saw, when I closed my eyes," she said softly. "Your face gave me strength, even when I just wanted it to be over. I wanted to get back to you more."

"Addy—" His voice broke, and he couldn't finish that sentence.

"Can you do something for me?" she asked, her voice sounding sleepy from her medication. Her skin was still too pale, and there were dark circles under her eyes. He'd tried to wash the blood out of her hair earlier with a damp towel and some water, but some of it had proven too stubborn. Her beauty still took his breath away.

"Anything you want, *mi amor*." He reached out for her, touched her face.

"Go to my house. You have the spare key." His confusion must have registered on his face, because she added, "There's something I need you to see."

"Now?"

"Right now," she said firmly. "Please."

He nodded. But as he rose to leave, she tugged on his sleeve. "Was Liz with you?"

"Yes."

She started to speak again, but he anticipated her. "She's fine. Took a bullet just above the knee, but she should be running again after a few months. She'll probably come down here as soon as they let her leave her room."

Relaxing back against the pillows, Addy pointed to the door. "You'd better get going."

He planted a soft kiss on her forehead and headed for Mermaid Point. When he finally reached her house, he wasn't prepared for what he saw upon entering.

It looked like Tijuana at Christmas in there, minus the tacky souvenirs. The candles and most of the photos in their black frames were gone, and in their place she'd put pretty much every sparkly, wildly colored, fuzzy and glittery thing she'd ever owned. Vases and bowls she'd painted or mosaiced in bright jewel tones covered every surface. A giant painting of a beautiful woman carrying a bouquet of multitoned wildflowers hung over the hearth, with Adriana's signature in hot pink in the bottom right corner. A horrible fuzzy throw in electric blue hung over the sofa, looking as if someone had attacked a Muppet to get it.

Okay, that might have to go. But the rest…

He moved through the house, slowly

drinking in every detail of every room. She'd scrubbed and polished, until the floor and furniture shone. And then she'd swept every sign of mourning and loss outside, opening her curtains as wide as they would go to let in the sunshine. In her bedroom, several cardboard boxes lined the wall—with Goodwill written on the side in marker. They were filled with black clothes.

As he made his way back to the front door, he paused next to the sofa table in the living room, which had formerly held at least ten photos of James Brentwood.

Now there was just one, in a mahogany and silver frame. It was a photo of the two of them together, walking on the beach and laughing.

Strangely enough, he was glad to see it there. God forbid if something happened to him, he hoped that she'd carry his memory in her heart, enough to keep at least one picture of him hanging around.

But he'd always do everything in his power to come home to her. Every night, from this night forward.

Then he noticed another frame lying flat beside the picture of Adriana and James. He picked it up, and saw it was a charcoal drawing.

Of his face.

He looked like a man in love.

All right, he looked like a total sap. But he had to admit, there was some truth to the image. That's what he was—a man in love.

He put the drawing down and practically ran out of the house.

In less than fifteen minutes, he was back at the hospital.

"That was quick," she said, using her elbows to sit up higher as he reentered her room.

"I used the sirens." In two strides he was back at her side, leaning down, and then he was kissing her sweet mouth and, oh, Lord, she was kissing him back.

Once they both came up for air, she put a hand up to caress the side of his face. "I wanted you to know—I meant what I said. James would want me to be happy. And you, Daniel Cardenas, make me very, very happy."

Why he always had this perverse impulse to bring up complications at times like this, he didn't know. But he had to ask. "Addy, I'm still a cop. I promise I will do everything, everything I can to come home to you, but there's a risk—"

"I'm a yoga instructor," she interrupted. "One bad downward dog and it's all over."

He laughed, his heart more full than he ever remembered it being.

She cupped his face with both hands, looking him right in the eye. “I love you,” she said. “Whether we have one more day or one hundred years ahead of us, I want to spend it with you. And I don’t want to be afraid.” And then she grimaced, her forehead wrinkling with worry. “That sounded needy, didn’t it? I really didn’t mean to sound—”

He stopped her words with a kiss. “Me, too,” he said. “I love you right back. Always.”

“I can’t believe that’s happened to me twice.” The smile she gave him was the most beautiful thing he’d ever seen.

* * * * *

Look for LAST WOLF WATCHING
by Rhyannon Byrd—the exciting conclusion
in the BLOODRUNNERS *miniseries*
from Silhouette Nocturne.

Follow Michaela and Brody on their fierce journey to find the truth and face the demons from the past, as they reach the heart of the battle between the Runners and the rogues.

Here is a sneak preview of book three, LAST WOLF WATCHING.

Michaela squinted, struggling to see through the impenetrable darkness. Everyone looked toward the Elders, but she knew Brody Carter still watched her. Michaela could feel the power of his gaze. Its heat. Its strength. And something that felt strangely like anger, though he had no reason to have any emotion toward her. Strangers from different worlds, brought together beneath the heavy silver moon on a night made for hell itself. That was their only connection.

The second she finished that thought, she knew it was a lie. But she couldn't deal with it now. Not tonight. Not when her whole world balanced on the edge of destruction.

Willing her backbone to keep her upright, Michaela Doucet focused on the towering blaze of a roaring bonfire that rose from the far side of the clearing, its orange flames burning with maniacal zeal against the inky black curtain of the night. Many of the Lycans had already shifted into their preternatural shapes, their fur-covered bodies standing like monstrous shadows at the edges of the forest as they waited with restless expectancy for her brother.

Her nineteen-year-old brother, Max, had been attacked by a rogue werewolf—a Lycan who preyed upon humans for food. Max had been bitten in the attack, which meant he was no longer human, but a breed of creature that existed between the two worlds of man and beast, much like the Bloodrunners themselves.

The Elders parted, and two hulking shapes emerged from the trees. In their wolf forms, the Lycans stood over seven feet tall, their legs bent at an odd angle as they stalked forward. They each held a thick chain that had been wound around their inside wrists, the twin lengths leading back into the shadows. The Lycans had taken no more than a few steps when they jerked on the chains, and her brother appeared.

Bound like an animal.

Biting at her trembling lower lip, she glanced left, then right, surprised to see that others had joined her. Now the Bloodrunners and their family and friends stood as a united force against the Silvercrest pack, which had yet to accept the fact that something sinister was eating away at its foundation—something that would rip down the protective walls that separated their world from the humans'. It occurred to Michaela that loyalties were being announced tonight—a separation made between those who would stand with the Runners in their fight against the rogues and those who blindly supported the pack's refusal to face reality. But all she could focus on was her brother. Max looked so hurt…so terrified.

"Leave him alone," she screamed, her soft-soled, black satin slip-ons struggling for purchase in the damp earth as she rushed toward Max, only to find herself lifted off the ground when a hard, heavily muscled arm clamped around her waist from behind, pulling her clear off her feet. "Damn it, let me down!" she snarled, unable to take her eyes off her brother as the golden-eyed Lycan kicked him.

Mindless with heartache and rage, Michaela clawed at the arm holding her, kicking her heels against whatever part of her captor's legs she could reach. "Stop it," a deep, husky voice grunted in her ear. "You're not helping him by losing it. I give you my word he'll survive the ceremony, but you have to keep it together."

"Nooooo!" she screamed, too hysterical to listen to reason. "You're monsters! All of you! Look what you've done to him! How dare you! *How dare you!*"

The arm tightened with a powerful flex of muscle, cinching her waist. Her breath sucked in on a sharp, wailing gasp.

"Shut up before you get both yourself and your brother killed. I will *not* let that happen. Do you understand me?" her captor growled, shaking her so hard that her teeth clicked together. "Do you understand me, Doucet?"

"Damn it," she cried, stricken as she watched one of the guards grab Max by his hair. Around them Lycans huffed and growled as they watched the spectacle, while others outright howled for the show to begin.

"That's enough!" the voice seethed in her ear. "They'll tear you apart before you even reach him, and I'll be damned if I'm going to stand here and watch you die."

Suddenly, through the haze of fear and agony and outrage in her mind, she finally recognized who'd caught her. *Brody.*

He held her in his arms, her body locked against his powerful form, her back to the burning heat of his chest. A low, keening sound of anguish tore through her, and her head dropped forward as hoarse sobs of pain ripped from her throat. “Let me go. I have to help him. *Please*,” she begged brokenly, knowing only that she needed to get to Max. “Let me go, Brody.”

He muttered something against her hair, his breath warm against her scalp, and Michaela could have sworn it was a single word… But she must have heard wrong. She was too upset. Too furious. Too terrified. She must be out of her mind.

Because it sounded as if he’d quietly snarled the word *never.*

Imagine a time of chivalrous knights and unconventional ladies, roguish rakes and impetuous heiresses, rugged cowboys and spirited frontierswomen— these rich and vivid tales will capture your imagination!

*Harlequin Historical . . .
they're too good to miss!*

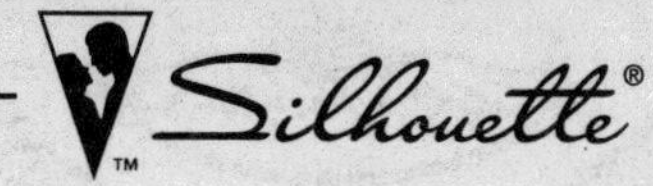

Silhouette®

SPECIAL EDITION™

Emotional, compelling stories that capture the intensity of living, loving and creating a family in today's world.

Modern, passionate reads that are powerful and provocative.

Silhouette®

nocturne

Dramatic and sensual tales of paranormal romance.

Romances that are sparked by danger and fueled by passion.

Visit Silhouette Books at www.eHarlequin.com

SDIR07